'You need ████████
Sally said ████████
moment a ████████
she shouldn't have a C-section
when the last doctor she spoke to
said she should!'

Tom frowned slightly. 'I talked to her when I scanned her. She was fine; she didn't say otherwise.'

'Verbally, perhaps not. But did you read her body language?' Sally's green eyes held his. 'She finds doctors intimidating. She was afraid to question you.'

Tom tensed, significantly discomforted by her implication that he'd been insensitive to the needs of a patient. But then why would Sally Jenner believe that he was capable of sensitivity?

He gritted his teeth and took the criticism on the chin. 'Believe it or not, I do try to interpret what women are feeling—'

He just wished he had seven years ago—and then Sally would still be his...

LAKESIDE MOUNTAIN RESCUE—

romance and drama that will keep you on the edge!

*Siblings Bryony, Tom and Oliver Hunter are
members of the Lakeside Mountain Rescue Team—
they're willing to risk all, ready to save lives!*

*And as winter approaches and
the weather worsens their skills, and their emotions,
are about to be tested to the limit...*

*Don't miss these three exciting novels
from Medical Romance™ starting with:*

THE DOCTOR'S CHRISTMAS BRIDE:
Bryony Hunter has been in love with A&E consultant
Jack Rothwell for most of her life, but to him she is his
best friend. So she decides that the time has come to
date other men. And suddenly Jack starts to see her in
a different light.

In **THE NURSE'S WEDDING RESCUE** meet GP
Oliver Hunter. He is waiting for Miss Right, but when
he finally meets her she's seriously on the rebound
after a disastrous break-up. How is he going to prove
to her that she can love again so soon?

This month in **THE MIDWIFE'S MARRIAGE
PROPOSAL** it's Tom's story. Tom Hunter broke up
with Sally Jenner seven years ago, to concentrate on
his career, and now she's back in his life. Despite the
uncontrollable passion between them, she makes it
clear that she isn't going to trust him with her heart
again. But Tom has other ideas...

THE MIDWIFE'S MARRIAGE PROPOSAL

BY

SARAH MORGAN

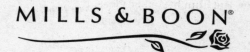

MILLS & BOON®

First published in Great Britain 2004
Paperback edition 2005
Harlequin Mills & Boon Limited,
Eton House, 18-24 Paradise Road, Richmond, Surrey TW9 1SR

© Sarah Morgan 2004

ISBN 0 263 84279 7

Set in Times Roman 10½ on 12 pt.
03-0105-46549

Printed and bound in Spain
by Litografía Rosés, S.A., Barcelona

PROLOGUE

SHE stood with her eyes on the mountains and her face to the wind, breathing in the smell of home.

It had been so long.

Too long.

She felt pressure on her arm and turned to her friend with an apologetic smile. 'Sorry.'

'For what?'

'For forgetting you were there.' Sally spread her arms and closed her eyes, letting the freezing air numb her cheeks and the biting wind whip her blonde hair into a tangled frenzy. 'It just feels so amazing to be back.'

No matter how far she'd travelled, how much of the world she'd explored, the Lake District had always been her home.

When pain and misery had almost destroyed her, she'd come here to seek comfort, and when circumstances had forced her to move away, she'd pined for the comfort of the fells.

'So why did you stay away so long?'

Sally's arms dropped to her sides and she whirled round, green eyes blazing. 'You know why.'

'Yes.' Bryony looked anguished. 'He drove you away.'

'He didn't. I chose to leave.' Sally's tone was steady and she caught a strand of hair that was blowing in front of her face, anchoring it with slender fingers. 'But now I'm back.'

And she was never leaving again.

'What made you come back now? After so long?'

Sally gave a wistful smile. 'I suppose I'd been thinking about it for a while and then I had your letter telling me that you'd finally married Jack and that Oliver had met someone.' She broke off, remembering how she'd felt when she'd read everything that had been happening at home. 'I suddenly realized how much I was missing my old friends. You are the nearest I have to family. I realized that it was time to come back.'

'He doesn't know, Sal.' Bryony's voice was quiet and Sally nodded.

That was exactly the way she'd planned it. If she was going to be able to hold herself together for that first, agonizing meeting, then she needed to be in a position of control.

'Thank you for not telling him.'

'Did you think I would?'

Sally shrugged, her expression guarded as she studied her childhood friend. 'He's your brother.'

'And you're my best friend.' Bryony gave a twisted smile. 'Or at least you *were* my best friend until Tom broke your heart and you vanished halfway round the world.'

'Friendships needn't be compromised by distance.'

Bryony bit her lip. 'I thought perhaps—' She shrugged her shoulders, showing how helpless she felt. 'I'm his sister, after all.'

Sally stirred. 'And you and I were best friends before he and I were lovers.'

'How will you—?' Bryony broke off and licked her lips. 'You're going to be working with him, Sally. Won't it be difficult for you?'

'No.' Sally lifted her chin, applying the rigid self-

discipline that she'd cultivated over the past seven years.
'It won't be difficult.'

Tom Hunter was part of her past. She'd learned to
live without him. His rejection had hurt her so badly that
for a while she'd thought she'd never recover. But she'd
put all that behind her. She'd built a new life, pushed
herself to the limits in a fevered determination never to
give herself time to stand still and contemplate. And in
the process she'd enjoyed experiences that to most people were just a dream. And developed a self-confidence
that had given her the courage to come home.

'I can't believe you applied for a job in his department.'

Sally gave a casual shrug. 'I'm a midwife, Bry, and
this is a small community. How many departments are
there?'

And it was part of the test she'd set herself. To see
how far she'd come in seven years.

'You could have gone to a different town.'

'No. This is my home,' Sally said softly, her eyes
fixed on the mountains with almost naked longing. 'And
I've stayed away long enough.'

And she'd pined for long enough.

Finally she'd picked up the pieces, stuck them back
together and made herself whole again.

She was ready to face the world.

And she was ready to face Tom Hunter.

CHAPTER ONE

'SALLY JENNER! I am so pleased to finally meet you.' Emma's smile was warm with welcome. 'I've heard such good things about you and we badly need an extra midwife. You are going to be everyone's most popular person.'

'Thanks. It's good to be here.' Sally smiled at the labour ward sister, but nothing could subdue the nervous fluttering in her stomach. The nerves had been there from the moment she'd made the decision to leave Australia and return home.

From the moment she'd known she would be seeing Tom Hunter again.

She'd prepared herself for this moment for seven years.

But now it was here she was suddenly terrified that she'd let herself down. Reveal something that she didn't want to reveal.

Feel something that she didn't want to feel.

What would he look like now? Had her memory exaggerated his masculine appeal? Could any man truly be the god she'd believed him to be?

'Anything you want to know, just ask me,' Emma said cheerfully, oblivious to Sally's anxiety. 'I know you trained in this hospital, but you've been away a while and some things might have changed so I'll give you a quick tour. We have two operating theatres, six traditional delivery rooms and four "home" rooms, as we call them. In other words, they're supposed to make people feel that they're actually in their own bedrooms.'

Sally laughed. 'You don't sound very convinced.'

'Well, my bedroom is buried under a ton of unwashed laundry and books that I intend to read at some point and haven't got round to yet,' Emma confessed cheerfully, 'so the rooms certainly don't look like *my* home. But I can dream.'

She pushed open a door and Sally followed her inside.

The room had a large double bed and a sofa covered in pretty scatter cushions. There were also magazines and a music system.

Sally gave a nod. 'Nice. Cosy.'

Emma shrugged. 'Well, it's a compromise between giving birth at home and in hospital. Now, come and see the birthing pool.'

They left the room and Emma opened another door and flicked on some lights. 'We have two, but the other one is in use at the moment.'

Sally walked into the room and looked at the pool. 'You do a lot of water births?' She knew that some of her medical colleagues had questioned the safety of water births. 'The consultants are comfortable with that?'

Emma gave a wry smile. 'Not all of them. The three older ones much prefer to just whip a woman into Theatre or yank the baby out with forceps the moment her labour starts to take longer than the books say it should. But attitudes are changing as younger consultants join the team.' She glanced over her shoulder and lowered her voice. 'I ought to warn you that if you're ever planning on having a baby here, Tom Hunter is your man. He's young but he's brilliant. He has amazingly good instincts and nerves of steel. Unlike some I could mention, he isn't frightened into C-sectioning everyone.' Her tone was warm. 'He thinks that a woman should be allowed to deliver by herself whenever possible and he does his best to let that happen.'

Sally slid a hand over the edge of the birthing pool, careful to hide her expression.

The knowledge that Tom was regarded as some sort of hero in the delivery suite clashed violently with her own negative attitude to the man.

She didn't want to admire him. It would make it even harder to manage her emotions.

'So he approves of the pool?'

'For labour, but not delivery,' Emma told her, leading the way out of the room and back down the corridor. 'He also approves of aromatherapy, relaxation techniques and breathing.'

Realizing that some sort of response was expected, Sally managed a smile. 'He sounds amazing.'

'He's very good with the women. Very skilled.'

Sally felt her insides twist viciously but kept her expression neutral. She knew exactly how skilled Tom Hunter was with women.

Swiftly she changed the subject. 'So I'll be working on the labour ward?'

'That's where we need you for now. We all move around the unit at times, and we try to give a woman a midwife that she knows, but you have a lot of labour ward experience and that's the most important thing.' Emma pushed open the door to the staffroom. 'And this is the most important room on the labour ward. Better take a good look. You won't get to see much of it.'

Sally walked over to the window and stared at the mountains, lost in their beauty, longing to be out there, walking or climbing. For her, life was a constant battle between her love of the outdoors and her love of midwifery.

She heard a heavy, male tread behind her and froze.

Even without looking she knew it was him.

She felt him.

They shared a connection that was beyond the physical. It had always been that way with them.

He'd truly been her other half. *Until he'd torn them apart.*

'Hi, Tom. You're just in time for a coffee and an introduction to our new midwife.' Emma's voice was bright and cheerful, like sunshine playing innocently in front of an approaching storm.

Reminding herself that she'd been rehearsing this exact moment for years, Sally turned, the expression in her green eyes cool and totally devoid of emotion as she brought into play all the skills she'd carefully developed.

He stood in the doorway, powerful legs spread apart in an arrogant pose, his blue eyes fixed on her with shimmering incredulity.

Sally felt the past slide over her like a suffocating cloak and with a determined effort she thrust it aside, reminding herself that the past was all about yesterdays and that she was only interested in today and tomorrow.

And neither was going to feature this man, even if he was straight out of a female fantasy.

And he was.

He'd always been indecently good-looking, she thought numbly, but age and maturity had added a hard edge to his masculinity that would make even the most cynical, man-wary female catch her breath.

And the combination of jet-black hair and blue eyes was a killer.

Resolutely she reined in her feelings, holding them close, reminding herself of the price of loving this man.

It was high. *Too high.*

She'd paid it once with interest and she wasn't prepared to pay it again.

So she held that dark gaze steadily and noted the shock that he couldn't quite conceal with a flicker of feminine satisfaction.

He hadn't expected her to come home.

But she had. And he was going to have to live with that.

Like it or not, she was back.

And she was staying.

'Hello, Tom.' Her voice was cool and formal. Not a tremor, not a shake, not a flicker of emotion. *She was proud of herself.* 'It's been a long time.'

Tom braced his shoulders and tried to counter the shock wave that pulsed through his body.

He'd always known that one day Sally Jenner would walk into his life again. That he'd be forced to stare his past in the face.

Acknowledge the guilt.

It had been seven years and yet he still wasn't able to remember their final encounter without breaking into a sweat.

He gritted his teeth, telling himself that he'd made the right decision for both of them, even though she hadn't been able to see it at the time.

At first glance she seemed hardly to have changed. Still the same intriguing green eyes that flashed a hint of rebellion and challenge, still the slim legs, the narrow waist and the delicate curves. She looked as though a strong gust of wind would blow her over, but he knew better. Sally was fit and strong, probably the most athletic woman he'd ever met. She was an accomplished rock-climber, an impressive long-distance runner, and her wildness and courage had stolen his heart. In all the years he'd known her, he'd seen her cry only once.

And that had been the day he'd ended their relationship.

Looking at her soft, perfectly shaped mouth, Tom suddenly had trouble remembering why he'd done it, and he cursed mentally, wishing that he'd had time to prepare himself for her arrival.

Why the hell hadn't someone told him that she was coming?

Warned him?

'Does Bryony know you're here?'

She'd been one of his sister's closest friends and he knew that they'd kept in touch over the years.

One delicate eyebrow lifted a fraction and he saw the challenge in her green gaze. 'Of course.'

He gritted his teeth. 'She failed to mention it.'

'She probably didn't think you'd be interested.'

It was a less than subtle reminder that he'd been the one to cut her out of his life and Tom ran a hand over the back of his neck, seriously discomfited for the first time in his thirty-four years.

If he'd known she was coming back, he would have had time to prepare—would have somehow arranged for them to have their first meeting in private. Clearly there were things that needed to be said.

As if reminding them both that they weren't alone, Emma gave a little cough.

'You know each other?' Her tone pulsed with a curiosity that she couldn't hide and she glanced between them with interest.

Sally smiled, nothing in her expression suggesting that she was anything other than totally relaxed. 'It was a long time ago.'

Her tone suggested a casual acquaintance of long standing, a relationship with no real attachment on either side.

Remembering the explosive passion they'd shared, Tom wondered how she'd managed to forget the incredible intimacies that had bound them together.

And then he looked into those cool green eyes and realized that she hadn't forgotten.

Neither had she forgiven.

In those green eyes he saw disdain where there had once been adoration, contempt where that had once been unconditional love.

He drew breath slowly, shocked by how severely that contempt unsettled him.

And yet what had he expected?

Had he known she was coming, how would he have anticipated their reunion?

Sally Jenner had every reason to hate him.

'I heard you were working in the Himalayas.' Suddenly he wanted to know everything about her. Where she'd been, what she'd been doing. *When she'd stopped crying over him.*

'Among other places.' Her reply was intentionally vague and he saw the flash in those green depths and understood.

Mind your own business, her eyes said. *What do you care, anyway?*

'And where are you living now?'

He needed to know. There were things he had to say to her and they certainly couldn't be said in public.

She ignored his question, her gaze turning to Emma

who was still watching them in awed silence. 'Sorry. This must be very boring for you and I'm sure we need to get on with some work.'

Emma shrugged. 'Well, if you two want to catch up, I can—'

'Not at all,' Sally interrupted her smoothly, moving away from the window and making her way towards the door. 'We've said hello. It was nice to see you, Tom.'

With a few casually spoken words she'd dismissed him as unimportant and Tom wrestled with an inexplicable impulse to power her against the wall and remind her just what they'd shared.

But that would be a totally illogical response, of course, given that he'd been the one to walk away from their relationship.

He'd thrown their relationship away. So why was he now questioning that decision?

Because in thirty-four years he'd never met another woman who stirred his blood like Sally Jenner.

It was only after she'd left the room that he realized that she hadn't said where she was living.

He narrowed his eyes. There was one person who would definitely know where she was living.

His sister, Bryony.

'I can't believe you know Tom,' Emma breathed as they walked back down the corridor. 'You didn't mention it when I talked about him.'

'It was a long time ago,' Sally said smoothly, wishing desperately that she could escape for just five minutes to gather together her scattered emotions. But there was no chance of that.

Almost as soon as they left the staffroom, one of the other midwives appeared, looking stressed.

'We've had two admissions in the last five minutes and one of them is Angela Norris. She's in a state.'

Emma gave a sigh and turned to Sally. 'Do you mind being thrown in at the deep end?' She gave a rueful smile. 'Angela isn't going to be easy to look after. She's only recently moved to the area and she's going to need a lot of care and attention. This is her second baby. The first was born by Caesarean section and she was promised a section again in her last hospital, but Tom isn't keen on sectioning women unless there's no alternative. He's told her that he wants her to aim for a normal delivery. She isn't very happy about the whole thing, to be honest.'

Sally felt her whole body tense. 'So...' She cleared her throat. 'Tom will be monitoring her?'

'Oh, yes—he'll keep a very close eye on her, especially if he's concerned about that scar.'

Which meant that she'd be working with him right from the start, with no chance to collect herself.

Sally closed her eyes briefly. What was the matter with her? She'd had seven years to collect herself. How much longer did she need? And she'd always known that taking a job in his department would mean working closely with him. She'd decided that she needed that. If only to prove to herself that she was over him. She'd decided to confront her fears head-on.

And she was going to be fine, she told herself firmly.

He was just a colleague, nothing more. A colleague.

'I'll be very happy to look after Angela,' she said firmly, smiling at Emma. 'Let's go.'

Angela was sitting on the bed in one of the rooms, her eyes red-rimmed from crying, a small suitcase at her feet. Her husband sat next to her, visibly tense as he held his wife's hand and tried to calm her down.

Sally was by her side in an instant, her expression concerned as she slipped an arm around the woman, the need to comfort instinctive in her. 'Don't be upset,' she urged softly, as she quickly introduced herself to the couple. 'Whatever the problem is, we'll sort it out together, I promise. This is supposed to be a happy, exciting time.'

Angela took a shuddering breath but her shoulders remained stiff under Sally's gentle touch. 'I really want a Caesarean section. It's what I had last time. It's what I was expecting. How can doctors say one thing in one place and something completely different in another? I just don't understand it.'

Her eyes filled again and Sally frowned slightly. 'I can see why that must be confusing, but the most important thing is to help you relax. Then we can talk about it.'

Angela fumbled for a tissue and blew her nose hard. 'I want a Caesarean,' she said emphatically, and Sally nodded.

'Can you tell me why?'

Angela closed her eyes and put a hand on her bump. 'Because it's safer. Oh, help, I've got another contraction coming.'

She screwed up her face and concentrated on her breathing while Sally encouraged her gently, smoothing her hand over the top of Angela's bump so that she could feel the strength of the contraction.

'That feels like a very strong contraction. Is it going off?' She felt the tightness ease under her hand and Angela nodded.

'Thankfully.' She drew in a deep breath and sighed. 'I didn't have any of this with my first one.'

Sally reached for the notes and skimmed them quickly. 'The baby was breech last time.'

'That's right. They told me I'd have to have a section right from the moment they found out, and the doctor told me at the time that if I had another baby that would be a section, too.'

'Having a section last time doesn't mean you can't have a normal delivery this time,' Sally said carefully, settling herself on the bed next to Angela. 'And it isn't necessarily safer, Angela. It depends on the circumstances. A Caesarean section is major abdominal surgery. Sometimes it's safer for you and the baby, but generally if you can give birth the normal way then that's preferable. Why don't we get you settled and then we can have a proper chat?'

Angela took several breaths. 'The doctor in my last hospital thought a section was the right thing for me. He said it was best.'

Sally took a deep breath. Best for whom? she wondered.

It was certainly true that some obstetricians were quicker to perform Caesareans than others, but the reasons for that weren't always as clear cut as they might be.

'All right,' she said firmly, 'this is what we're going to do. I can completely understand that it must be very confusing for you having come from a hospital saying one thing to a hospital saying another...'

Angela looked at her. 'And I don't know anyone here,' she muttered. 'We had to move here because of Peter's job. I knew all the midwives at the hospital in London. Here I don't know anyone.'

Her husband looked racked with guilt. 'I should never have taken the job.'

Angela sighed and brushed her hair out of her eyes. 'It's a good job, and you've always wanted to live here.'

'A sensible man. This is a great place to live,' Sally said lightly, taking Angela's hand in hers and squeezing it firmly. 'I'll tell you a secret. I don't know anyone either. I'm a very experienced midwife but this is my first day on this particular unit so we can bond together and keep each other company.'

Angela gave a wobbly smile. 'But you'll go off duty before the baby is born.'

Sally shook her head. 'Not me. All that's waiting for me at home is lots of unpacking and even more washing so, trust me on this, I'm looking for an excuse to stay at the hospital.'

'Unpacking?'

'I've been away for a while,' Sally said with a smile. 'I haven't had a chance to settle back in yet.'

Emma cleared her throat. 'I'll leave the two of you together.' She looked at Sally. 'I'll let Mr Hunter know that Angela is here.'

Angela sighed. 'He's the one who wants me to have it the normal way.'

Her husband took a deep breath. 'The guy has a brilliant reputation, Angela. I've talked to a few people about him. I think you should listen to what he has to say.'

Sally was reading the notes again. 'I agree with your husband. You need to have a proper talk with him, tell him how you feel.'

'I'm useless with doctors,' Angela mumbled. 'They always intimidate me. Before they arrive in my room I have all these questions, and then once they're standing there I can't bring myself to ask any of them.'

'Well I'll be with you,' Sally assured her, 'and I'll

make sure that he answers all your questions and that you don't feel intimidated. Let me know when you have another contraction because I want to listen to the baby's heart.'

Angela screwed up her face and sucked in a breath. 'I've got another pain coming now.'

Sally reached for the Sonicaid and the sound of the baby's heartbeat echoed around the room.

'That's sounding good. Remember your breathing. That's it. Great…' Sally coached her gently, timing the contraction, and when Angela finally relaxed again she stood up. 'Right. I'd like to examine you and see how your labour is progressing, and then I'm going to hook you up to one of our machines just for a short while. Then we'll find Mr Hunter.'

And that was the bit that she wasn't looking forward to.

Tom finished writing up a set of notes and glanced up to find Sally standing there.

His whole body tightened and he rose to his feet, his eyes fixed to hers.

For a moment they stared at each other, the clinical nature of their surroundings forgotten, tension pulsing between them like a living force.

Then she dragged her eyes away from his and took a deep breath.

'I need to talk to you about Angela.' Her tone was cool and professional, not a hint of the personal in her manner. 'I've examined her and she's four centimetres dilated, but it sounds as though she's been in labour for a while. She's very anxious. Her last obstetrician said that he was going to section her.'

His brain registered the fact that she was talking about

work but the rest of his body was concentrating on something entirely different. His attention was caught by her seductively long lashes and by the fullness of her perfect mouth.

He'd been the first man to kiss that mouth.

The first man to—

With a determined effort he pulled himself together. 'I'm not planning to section her. I scanned her two weeks ago to measure the thickness of the lower uterine segment and I was perfectly satisfied that she's a good candidate for vaginal delivery this time round.'

'Then you need to talk to her,' Sally said calmly. 'Because at the moment all she's hearing is contradiction, and she has no reason to believe you are any more skilled than the last man she spoke to.'

Tom frowned slightly. 'I talked to her when I scanned her. She was fine.'

'She was confused and worried.'

'She didn't say anything.'

'Verbally, perhaps not. But did you read her body language?' Her eyes held his. 'She finds doctors intimidating. She was afraid to question you.'

Tom tensed, significantly discomfited by her implication that he'd been insensitive to the needs of a patient.

But, then, why would Sally believe that he was capable of sensitivity?

He gritted his teeth and took the criticism on the chin. 'Believe it or not, I do try to interpret what women are feeling. I certainly don't want them worried by anything I've said.'

'Well, she's worried,' Sally said flatly, 'and at the moment she is totally convinced that what she needs is another C-section.'

Tom inhaled sharply. 'Caesarean rates have been

steadily increasing over the last two decades,' he said harshly. 'Eighty per cent of women can safely deliver vaginally after a previous section, providing they meet certain criteria.'

Her gaze didn't flicker. 'I'm well aware of that.' Her voice was smoky and soft and curled around his raw emotions like the smoothest silk. 'All I'm saying is that she'd been told she was having another Caesarean and then you told her she wasn't, and she didn't understand how two doctors could say such different things. She deserves an explanation. In fact, I'd go as far as to say she needs an explanation, otherwise she will be far too anxious to concentrate on her labour. She's stressed and I'm sure you're aware of the evidence that suggests that stress can reduce uterine activity.'

He listened, intrigued by the change he saw in her.

This wasn't the Sally he'd known.

When had she developed such poise and confidence? he wondered, his eyes sliding over the determined jut of her chin and the set of her narrow shoulders. He could remember clearly a time when she'd hung on to his every word as if he were some sort of god. When she'd been so lacking in self-confidence that she'd barely been able to make a decision without help.

Now she stood her ground, challenging him to defend his decision without displaying a flicker of discomfort, every bit his equal.

'I'll talk to her,' he said finally, slipping his pen into his pocket and closing the notes in which he'd been writing. 'We'll do it together. Then you can tell me if I'm insensitive.'

He strolled round the desk and saw her back away hastily, as if she was afraid that he might touch her.

The realization that he wanted to do just that came as a shock.

For a moment their eyes held, and if they hadn't been standing in the middle of the labour ward, in full view of anyone who happened to pass, Tom would have kissed that soft mouth that he remembered so well.

He'd been addicted to her mouth. The look of it, the feel of it under his, *the taste of it*…

'We need to talk, Sally,' he said roughly. 'In private.'

In fact, he realized with a sudden stab of shock that he wanted to do a great deal more than talk.

Something flickered in those green depths. 'No.' Her voice was low but firm and she glanced over her shoulder quickly, as if she was afraid someone might have overheard his comment. 'We don't need to talk.'

Tom drew in a long breath, finding it difficult to know how to respond to this new, confident Sally.

In the old days she would have talked.

In the old days she couldn't get enough of him.

They'd talked for hours about everything and anything.

'All right, then, I'll talk and you can just listen. There are things I need to say to you.'

They couldn't pretend that the past hadn't happened.

If they were going to be able to work together effectively, then at the very least they needed to clear the air.

She looked at him. 'You said everything that needed to be said on the last occasion we met.' Her gaze was clear and direct and her voice was remarkably steady. 'And I got your message, Tom. Loud and clear.'

CHAPTER TWO

SALLY turned and walked back along the corridor, her legs shaking and her heart thumping.

When she'd imagined meeting him again, part of her had wondered whether she would feel differently about Tom. Didn't people often look back and wonder what they'd seen in their first love? She'd often wondered if that would be true of her. Would she look at Tom and wonder what all the fuss had been about?

But now she knew that the answer to that was no.

She could see exactly why she'd fallen for Tom and she knew that if she wasn't careful, she could fall for him again.

He was the sexiest man alive, with those sharp blue eyes, that brilliant brain and that unshakable self-confidence that had been such a draw when she'd been an insecure teenager.

He'd always been strong in every sense of the word and he was still strong.

Reminding herself that she wasn't insecure any more and that she didn't need his strength, she lifted a hand to push open the door to Angela's room, but a powerful arm slid in front of her and turned her round, backing her against the wall.

'Don't think you can avoid me for ever,' Tom warned softly, his blue eyes burning into hers as he planted an arm to one side of her, reducing her opportunities for escape. 'You chose to come back.'

He was too close.

She couldn't cope when he was this close.

Her nose picked up the tantalizing male smell that was Tom, and desire, long dormant, uncoiled low in her pelvis.

She flattened herself against the wall, impossibly aware of the strength in his shoulders and the hardness of his eyes.

'What are you implying?' Her eyes sparked into his and she pushed the past to the front of her brain. *She wasn't doing this again.* 'That I came back to you? Don't flatter yourself, Tom. I came back home. My friends are here. Friends I've missed. I have as much right to live here as you.'

The fact that her friends were also his friends and family was something that she didn't want to think about right now.

In fact, she couldn't think about anything much with him standing so close to her.

She wanted to move but she couldn't.

Her body was pinned against the wall, trapped by the heat of his gaze and by her own weakness.

'Which is why we need to talk. This is a small community, Sally. Everyone knows about our past relationship. Do you really think it's something that we can ignore? We need to deal with it.'

She was painfully aware of the warmth and power of his body so close to hers, of the fact that if she moved even a fraction she would be in his arms.

And that was the last place in the world she wanted to be.

Suddenly she found the strength she needed.

'We both dealt with it seven years ago, Tom,' she said calmly, her steady voice totally at odds with the rapid beating of her heart, 'and people will soon get used to the idea that our relationship is purely professional now. Excuse me. I need to get back to Angela.'

His eyes narrowed slightly but his arm dropped and he stood to one side.

Feeling totally shaken but determined not to show it, Sally walked into the room and smiled at the woman now comfortably settled on the bed.

'How are you doing, Angela? I've brought Mr Hunter to have a word with you.' Desperate for a few moments to collect her thoughts and calm her frantic pulse rate, she checked the CTG trace carefully. Then she glanced at Tom, her expression neutral, as if he were a consultant she'd only just met and not a man who had been the love of her life. 'Do you want her to be continuously monitored?'

Tom shook his head. 'Not for the time being. There's no reason for it, providing we keep a close eye on everything.' He smiled at Angela and settled himself on the edge of the bed. 'It seems as though I owe you an apology.' His voice was soft and his eyes shone with warmth as he looked at the anxious woman. 'When I saw you a few weeks ago I told you that I wanted you to try and deliver this baby yourself. I obviously didn't notice how worried you were.'

Angela shifted awkwardly. 'It doesn't matter...'

'It matters,' Tom said firmly, 'and from now on I need you to promise that you'll ask me about anything that worries you and we'll talk about it together. Do you promise?'

Angela looked at him and a smile wobbled on her face. 'All right.'

'Good.' Tom nodded and took the CTG trace that Sally handed him, his gaze flickering over the paper, interpreting the results. Then he handed the paper back to her and took a deep breath. 'Let's talk about Caesarean sections,' he said quietly. 'There are a few things that I should explain. It's a major operation, Angela, and it is not the ideal way to have a baby if there are alternatives. When you had your first child, clearly the doctors thought that a section was the safest mode of delivery, but this time I think you should deliver vaginally.'

Angela licked dry lips. 'And what if I can't?'

'I'm very confident that you can or I wouldn't be suggesting it,' Tom said calmly, 'but Sally and I will be with you every step of the way, and if anything about your labour suggests that a Caesarean would be safer then I'll section you.'

Angela glanced nervously at her husband. 'We've read about uterine rupture…'

Tom nodded. 'All right, let's talk about that.' His voice was deep and confident. 'Firstly you should know that it is a very rare occurrence.'

'But it does happen.'

'It can do,' Tom admitted, 'which is why we very carefully select the women who we think can deliver vaginally after a section. The chance of a successful delivery is lowered if labour is induced, but you've gone into spontaneous labour so that's good. I've also taken into account the type of incision that your obstetrician used last time and the way that the uterus was repaired. All of that makes me confident that you can deliver vaginally.'

Angela shifted slightly on the bed. 'So why did my last consultant want me to have another section?'

Tom hesitated and it was Angela's husband who answered.

'I suppose doctors have different opinions about

what's best,' he said gruffly, 'but it seems to me that Mr Hunter is talking sense. And you know how sad you were not to have the baby naturally last time. You said as much at the time.'

Angela nodded. 'I know.' She put her hand on her scar protectively. 'But I don't want anything to go wrong.'

Tom took her hand. 'I know you're anxious, Angela,' he said softly, 'but I'm asking you to trust me. And to trust Sally.' He glanced at her with a warm smile, nothing in his gaze suggesting that they were anything other than the closest of colleagues. 'Sally will be with you the whole time and I will be popping in and out during the day. If we're remotely concerned, we'll think again, but I want us to aim for a vaginal delivery.'

He was confident and totally in control and Sally saw Angela relax.

It was a shame he didn't have the same effect on her, she reflected helplessly. The closer Tom was, the tenser she became.

Angela gave a gasp as another contraction tore through her body and Sally waited for Tom to move so that she could sit with the mother and help her through it.

But he didn't move. Instead, he placed a hand on the top of the mother's uterus and felt the contraction, talking to Angela softly as he did so, encouraging her to breathe properly, reminding her what her body was doing.

Angela screwed up her face and grabbed Tom's arm, her fingers digging hard into his flesh, but he didn't flinch.

Sally watched him helplessly, part of her wanting him to do something wrong just so that it would be easier to hate him. She knew he could be hard and insensitive. She'd been on the receiving end of his ruthless streak. She didn't want to see his soft side. Didn't want to see any single part of him that made him attractive.

'Good girl.' His voice was warm with approval as he spoke quietly to Angela. 'That was a strong contraction. You're coping very well.'

Flushed from his praise and encouragement, Angela let out a long breath. 'But I haven't dilated much. If I don't hurry up, are you going to induce me?'

Tom shook his head and stood up. 'In this hospital, Angela, we meddle with nature as little as possible and with as much subtlety as possible. If I induce you, your contractions will be even stronger and that will put more strain on the uterus. For the time being we're leaving it all to nature, but obviously we'll be watching closely to make sure she doesn't have any surprises in mind. Have you considered pain relief?'

'No.' Angela shook her head and glanced anxiously at her husband. 'Because I thought I was having a section. I suppose I should just have an epidural.'

'You could do that,' Tom agreed, 'but epidurals are not without their drawbacks. Why don't you start off by trying our pool?'

Angela looked at him. 'You mean a water birth?'

'I'd rather you didn't actually deliver in the water,' Tom said, 'but it's certainly an excellent way of relaxing. Would you like to give it a try? Many women find that being in the water really helps them cope with the pain.'

Angela glanced at her husband and then nodded. 'All right. Yes, I think I'd like that. I always fancied the idea but with the first one I always knew I was having a section from the start and so I didn't think it would ever be an option for me.'

Tom smiled. 'Well, it's an option now. I'll get someone to get one of our pools ready.' He turned to Sally. 'Any problems, call me. I'll have a word with Emma.'

With that he strode out of the room, leaving them all staring after him.

'He's nice,' Angela said immediately, shifting on the bed to try and find a more comfortable position. 'Very confident. The sort of person you feel you can depend on.'

Sally moved the CTG machine out of the way, careful to mask her own feelings. She'd certainly depended on Tom a great deal. In fact, he'd been her whole life, and when he'd ended their relationship...

She pushed the memories aside and settled herself next to Angela. She wasn't going to think about Tom. She was going to do her job and settle back down at home.

'Do you have any children?' Angela looked at her and Sally shook her head.

'No. I'm not married.'

Angela laughed and rubbed her swollen stomach. 'As if that makes a difference these days. Do you want children of your own?'

Once she'd wanted that more than anything else in the world.

Sally smiled. 'One day, maybe,' she said quietly, glancing over her shoulder with relief as Emma stuck her head round the door.

'The pool's ready for you. I've brought you a wheel-chair.'

'Thanks, Emma.' Sally slid a hand over Angela's

uterus. 'We'll wait until after the next contraction and then we'll make a move.'

Four hours later Angela was progressing well.

'I love the water,' she moaned softly, closing her eyes and breathing carefully as another contraction hit her. 'It feels so soothing. And I love being able to move around.'

Sally checked the baby's heart with the underwater Doppler, satisfied that everything seemed to be going well.

'Why do you keep listening after the contraction ends?' Angela's husband had been by her side the whole way through, asking questions constantly.

Respecting his concern, given their previous experience, Sally had been careful to give him detailed answers to everything.

'During a contraction blood can't flow through the placenta so easily. Some babies are fine with that, but others may not be and their heart rate may be affected. It's a sign that the baby is stressed. If it happens in the middle of the contraction and the baby's heart recovers quickly, we don't worry too much, but if a baby's heart rate is affected after the contraction is finished then we need to keep an eye on it.'

He stroked a hand over his wife's head and offered her a glass of water. 'But in our case everything is fine?'

'Absolutely.' Sally removed the Doppler from the water and dried her hands. She had been monitoring Angela like a hawk, constantly alert to any signs that her scar might be threatening to rupture. 'How are you doing, Angela?'

'Fine. I love the water. I'm just anxious about what's to come.'

There was a tap on the door and Tom strolled into the room dressed in theatre scrubs.

The loose cotton fabric emphasized the width and strength of his shoulders and revealed a tantalizing glimpse of dark chest hair.

Sally swallowed and concentrated her attention on Angela. She'd always adored his body. He was the most masculine man she'd ever met and she'd never been able to look at him without feeling her stomach lurch.

It seemed that nothing had changed.

She didn't want to feel like this.

Hadn't expected to feel like this.

Seven years of absence was supposed to have cured her of Tom Hunter.

She closed her eyes for a second, trying to blot out the vision of those strong arms and that firm mouth, resenting the pull of attraction that tugged at her body.

She breathed in deeply and tried to focus her mind.

Better to acknowledge the attraction and control it than deny it and allow it free rein to consume her.

All right, so she was still physically attracted to him. Who wouldn't be?

It didn't mean that she was going to be stupid enough to fall for him again.

There was no way she'd risk exposing herself to that degree of pain a second time.

Clearly oblivious to her internal battle, Tom walked across the room, his eyes on Angela.

'How's it going?' His voice was velvety smooth and he crouched down by the pool, his eyes warm as they rested on the labouring mother. Despite having a punishing workload, he'd been in and out of the room all afternoon, checking on Angela and getting updates from Sally.

And Sally had to admit that he was good. Because he'd bothered to spend the time, Angela was now totally relaxed with him, and it was obvious that she trusted Tom implicitly.

'All right, I think—' Angela sucked in a breath and gave him a weak smile. 'Not looking forward to the end bit, to be honest. I'm just worried that Sally will leave me and go home if I take too long.'

Sally smiled. 'I'm not going anywhere.'

Home was Bryony's cottage. A lonely reminder that she didn't actually have anywhere that was hers.

But she'd sort that out, given the first opportunity.

She was off at the weekend and she'd already made arrangements to view a couple of places.

Angela looked at Tom. 'She's brilliant. So calm. Better than pain relief. Everyone in labour should have Sally.'

Tom looked at Sally and she saw something flicker in his blue gaze. 'I agree,' he said softly, 'Sally is very special.'

But not special enough to prevent him from ending their relationship.

Flattened by painful memories, Sally straightened and walked over to the flickering candles that she'd lit earlier in an attempt to help Angela relax.

Tom followed her. 'You're happy with her?' His eyes were searching and she nodded, looking away quickly from that disturbing blue gaze.

When he'd made love to her she'd always stared into his eyes. Had been unable to take her eyes off him, hypnotized by the wonder of being with Tom. Looking into his eyes had been the only way she'd been able to believe that she'd actually been living the fantasy. That this amazing man had wanted her.

And when he hadn't wanted her any more she'd almost died.

The reduced lighting and his low voice created an atmosphere of such intimacy that she felt the breath lodge in her throat. It was the cruellest reminder of what they'd once shared.

She had to remind herself that they were standing in a delivery room with a labouring woman and she was suddenly tempted to blow out the candles and turn on every fluorescent light in the room.

'The foetal heart rate is good and she's contracting regularly. No tachycardia or any other signs that her uterus is in any way compromised.'

Tom nodded. 'Good.'

'Sally!' Angela's tone was suddenly sharp and panicky. 'I want to push. All of a sudden…'

Sally was by her side in an instant, Tom forgotten. 'Don't panic,' she said quietly, reaching for some towels that were warming. 'I'm going to get you out of the water and examine you again. You weren't even eight centimetres last time we checked so I doubt you've dilated that quickly.'

Angela groaned and clutched the side of the pool, her eyes tightly closed. 'Can't I stay in?'

Sally glanced at Tom but he gave a slight shake of his head. 'I'd rather you had this particular baby on dry land.'

Angela gasped. 'I don't think I can move.'

'Wait until this contraction has passed and then we'll help you out.'

A few minutes later Angela was lying on the bed, wrapped in a warm dressing-gown.

Sally snapped on a pair of gloves. 'Don't push,

Angela. I'm just going to see what's happening. I don't want you pushing until your cervix is fully dilated.'

'I definitely want to push.' Angela gave a gasp and stopped dead, her fingers biting into Sally's arm. 'Oh…'

Tom frowned. 'How dilated was she when she went into the pool?'

'Four centimetres.' Sally examined her carefully and then straightened up. 'Obviously all that warm water and relaxation did the trick. You're fully dilated, Angela, and the baby is nicely positioned. You can push whenever you like.'

She looked at Tom expectantly, wondering whether he intended to deliver the baby himself, but he gave a shake of his head.

'Your delivery,' he said softly, a faint smile on his hard mouth. 'Obstetricians only get involved if they have to, and everything is looking fine from my point of view. But I intend to hang around and watch.'

Just in case something went wrong.

Ignoring that smile, Sally turned her attention back to Angela just as Emma popped her head round the door.

'Do we have action?'

Angela gave a gasp and her husband stepped forward and took her hand.

'Go on, abuse me,' he groaned. 'This is all my fault.'

Angela gave a tired laugh. 'You can say that again. You and your stupid ideas. ''Wouldn't it be great to have another child?'' were your exact words.'

'Next time I say that you have full permission to hit me,' her husband said, his tone full of remorse as he stroked Angela's hair away from her damp forehead. 'What can I do?'

'Just be there.' Angela closed her eyes and screwed

up her face as another contraction hit and she pushed. 'Oh—I never thought it would hurt this much!'

Sally showed her how to use the gas and air properly and Angela breathed in steadily.

Emma was by her side. 'Do you need me, or are you staying, Mr Hunter?'

'I want him to stay,' Angela said quickly, her breath coming in pants. 'Please, Mr Hunter. If something goes wrong, I want you to be there.'

'Nothing is going to go wrong,' Tom said, his voice deep and reassuring. But he didn't leave the room. Instead, he lifted an eyebrow at Sally and Emma. 'Well, if I'm becoming a midwife, you'd better give me some instructions.'

'You can take the baby,' Sally said stiffly, looking away from his disturbingly intense blue gaze and turning her attention back to the mother. 'Well done, Angela. Won't be long now.'

Angela gave a gasp. 'Do I need to lie down? I don't want to make it awkward for you.'

'You can deliver in any position that feels comfortable to you,' Sally assured her, adjusting her own position so that she could see what was happening more clearly.

'I've got another contraction coming…'

'It's crowning,' Sally said softly. 'You're doing so well, Angela. Try not to push now. I just want you to pant. Pretend you're blowing out a candle, that's it—great.'

Moments later Sally had safely delivered the head. She checked that the cord wasn't around the baby's neck and shifted her position slightly. 'We'll wait for the next contraction, Angela,' she said, 'and then this baby will be born.'

But it wasn't.

The contraction came and Angela pushed again, but nothing happened.

With a feeling of unease, Sally encouraged Angela to change position but still nothing happened and she was aware that Tom had pulled on a pair of sterile gloves.

He nudged her to one side.

'I want you to change position one more time for me, Angela.' His voice was confident and reassuring as he explained what he wanted her to do. 'I need you more upright—that's it. It widens your pelvic outlet. And now I'm going to see if I can give this baby a hand.'

He worked his fingers carefully inside, did something that Sally couldn't quite see and the baby came slithering out into his hands with an outraged yell.

'You have a son, Angela.' His voice was calm and relaxed. 'Congratulations.'

'Oh.' Angela plopped down onto the bed, her expression dazed and delighted. 'What happened then? What did you do?'

'I didn't do anything,' Tom said easily, handing her the baby carefully. 'You did it all yourself. You were brilliant. Does it feel good?'

Angela stared down at the tiny baby in her arms and her eyes filled. 'Yes.' Her voice was a whisper. 'It feels great.'

Sally blinked back tears and then cursed to herself as Tom gave her a searching look.

Bother. She always found childbirth emotional but the last thing she wanted to do was show that emotion in front of Tom.

An hour later, having handed Angela and her baby son over to the nurse from the ward, Sally went and picked up her bag and coat from the staffroom.

She felt totally exhausted.

It had been a long day, but she knew that it wasn't the work that had left her feeling drained.

It was seeing Tom again.

She found deliveries emotional at the best of times, and having Tom working shoulder to shoulder with her on her very first day had left her shaken and tense. What she really needed was to climb. Climbing always relaxed her. It was the degree of concentration required, the knowledge that to allow the mind to wander for one second might result in a fall.

She stared out of the window, acknowledging the dark. It was too late to climb.

So she would need to find another way to escape. She needed to look elsewhere for relaxation and distraction from Tom.

She slid her arms into her coat and made for the door, her whole body tensing when she saw him standing there.

Her defences rose and her chin lifted. 'Excuse me.'

'No.' He walked in and closed the door behind him, standing with his back to her only escape route. 'I won't let you avoid me, Sally.'

'I can hardly be accused of avoiding you,' she said lightly. 'I've been working side by side with you for most of the day.'

'And it's been torture, hasn't it?' His voice was harsh and he breathed in deeply. 'We need to talk about the past. About what happened between us. And we need to move on.'

'It was seven years ago. And I've already moved on.' She clutched her bag in front of her like a shield. 'There is absolutely nothing to talk about. I can barely remember it.'

She shot him a look of pure indifference, one of the many looks that she'd been practising.

'Is that so?' His voice was soft and his blue eyes narrowed as he surveyed her. He was trying to penetrate that shield but her armour was strong, forged from the burning fires of pain and betrayal.

'The past is just a memory,' she lied smoothly, 'and memories are easily forgotten over time.'

'Well, you may have nothing to say on the subject, but I have plenty.'

'Then that's your problem, not mine. And now I'm going home. It's been a long day.' She walked up to him and lifted her chin, her eyes flashing into his. 'Excuse me.'

There was a tense moment when she thought he was going to reach for her, but then the door behind him opened and he was forced to step aside.

Emma stuck her head round. 'Oh, great, you're still here.' She smiled at Sally. 'Bryony is on the phone. She said to tell you that she's in the car park if you want a lift home.'

'Thanks.' Without glancing in Tom's direction, Sally walked confidently out of the room, casting a smile at Emma. 'See you tomorrow.'

She didn't want to talk to him. Didn't want an intimate conversation. She just wanted him to treat her as a colleague, nothing more.

That was all she could cope with.

CHAPTER THREE

TOM watched the staffroom door close behind the two women and fought the temptation to put his fist through the window.

He was boiling with frustration, aggravated to the point of explosion by the less than satisfactory exchange with Sally. There were things he needed to say and she wasn't allowing him to say them.

But could he really blame her for that?

He ran a hand over his face and cursed softly. All day he'd been aware of her and it had disturbed his concentration more than he cared to admit.

She'd always played havoc with his emotions.

He prowled over to the window and stared moodily down into the car park, his jaw tightening as he saw Sally opening the door of his sister's car and sliding inside.

He saw a flash of long leg, a glimmer of blonde hair and then she vanished from sight.

For now.

He comforted himself with the fact that Sally Jenner wasn't going anywhere. She'd made the decision to come home so she was obviously planning on staying around. Which meant that he had plenty of time to engineer the conversation he was determined to have.

His mouth tightened as he watched Bryony drive off.

And the first thing he was going to do was talk to his sister.

* * *

Sally settled into her seat and gave a self-satisfied smile. 'Thanks for the lift. Excellent timing. It's hard to make a dramatic exit on a mountain bike.'

Bryony caught the smile and laughed. 'From the look on your face, I gather you won that round.'

Sally took a steady breath. 'Well, I didn't make a fool of myself. You would have been proud of me. I was Miss Cool.'

And somehow she'd managed to pretend an indifference that she hadn't felt.

Seeing Tom had affected her even more than she'd imagined it would.

Bryony waited for her to fasten her seat belt and then drove off. 'I would have liked to have seen his face when he saw you.'

'He was shocked,' Sally said softly, recalling the look in his eyes with a slight shiver. 'And disconcerted, I think.'

'Never seen my big brother disconcerted about anything before,' Bryony said dryly, shifting gears and slowing down as she approached the exit of the hospital. 'I wish I could have been there.'

'Well, fortunately Emma was,' Sally told her. 'That wasn't a meeting I would have wanted to have in private.'

'So what did he say?'

Sally moistened dry lips. 'He wants to talk.'

Bryony paused at the junction, her expression serious. 'About what?'

'The past, I suppose.' Her eyes met her friend's and Bryony pulled a face.

'Well, that was to be expected.'

'I don't want to talk about it, Bry. It was bad enough when it happened, without reliving it. What can we possibly achieve by talking about it?' Sally asked hoarsely, pulling her coat around herself with a slight shiver. 'Can you turn the heating up in this car? It's freezing.'

'The engine will warm up in a minute,' Bryony said absently, checking the traffic and pulling onto the main road. 'And you know as well as I do that if my big brother sets his mind on something, he gets it.'

Sally lifted her chin and stared into the frosty darkness. 'I can be as determined as him.'

In the past seven years she'd discovered reservoirs of strength in herself that she hadn't known existed.

She wasn't the same person who had run for cover when he'd rejected her.

Bryony sighed. 'I know. Which means we're in for fireworks.' She gave her a sympathetic glance. 'You may not want to talk, but if it's what Tom wants then, trust me, you'll be talking. He isn't easily distracted when he wants something. You know that as well as I do.'

Of course she did.

It was that same single-minded approach that had made him such a respected obstetrician at such a young age.

Bryony sighed. 'You'll be fine, Sally. You've put him behind you.'

A long silence greeted her words and Bryony glanced at her friend in consternation. 'Oh, no, tell me you're not…'

'No.' Sally's voice sounded croaky and she cleared her throat. 'No, I'm not. But it was hard, Bry. Really hard. Even harder than I thought it would be.'

And she'd always known that seeing Tom again would be difficult.

Bryony reached out and squeezed her hand. 'Just take

it a day at a time. What you need is a new love interest. I'm going to find you someone gorgeous to help take your mind off my brother.'

Sally shook her head. 'No, thanks. I'm better off on my own.'

'Can I ask you something?' Bryony pulled up outside her old cottage and switched off the engine. 'Has there been anyone since Tom?'

Sally turned away, her eyes fixed out of the window. 'Let's just say he was a hard act to follow.' She gave a sigh and then turned to Bryony with a bright smile. 'But I'm working on it. Truly.'

Somewhere out there was a man who wouldn't seem like second best.

She sat, lost in thought, and the silence stretched into infinity.

Finally Bryony spoke. 'Are you truly going to be able to move on?' Her tone was doubtful and Sally stirred.

'I've moved on. I'm home,' she said simply, undoing her seat belt and reaching for her bag. Suddenly she needed to be on her own. 'Thanks for lending me the cottage. I'll find somewhere of my own soon.'

'No need,' Bryony said with a frown. 'Jack and I don't use it any more. We were going to rent it out anyway. Does Tom know you're staying here?'

Sally paused with her hand on the doorhandle. 'No. He asked where I was living but I dodged the question.'

'But it isn't going to take him long to figure it out. What if he comes here?'

'I hardly think he's going to go to those lengths to have a conversation,' Sally said with a faint smile. 'Goodnight, Bry. Thanks for the lift.'

'You left your bike at the hospital,' Bryony reminded her. 'I'll pick you up in the morning.'

Smiling her thanks. Sally let herself into the cottage, flicked on the lights and walked through to the cosy kitchen, feeling the tension in her neck and shoulders.

It had been a hard day. Harder than she'd anticipated.

She'd known that the first meeting would be difficult, of course. Known that seeing Tom would be painful.

She'd expected to feel anger and contempt. Expected to dismiss him with a few well-rehearsed words.

What she hadn't anticipated had been the race of her heart and the kick of her breathing.

Sally made herself a coffee and then sat down at the kitchen table, her hands coiled round the hot mug.

Tom Hunter was still a dangerously attractive man.

But he had no place in her life any more.

She wasn't that careless with her heart.

Tom sat in his sister's kitchen, tapping long fingers on the table.

'She'll be home in a minute, but I probably ought to warn you that you're not flavour of the month,' Jack said mildly, opening two beers and handing one to his friend.

Tom drank from the bottle and then banged it down on the table. 'Did you know Sally was back?'

Jack settled himself opposite, his feet on the table. 'No. If Bry wanted to keep it from you, she's hardly going to tell me, is she?'

'You're her husband.'

Jack grinned. 'And you and I have been best mates since primary school, Tom. Takes more than a woman to come between us, even if that woman is your sister.'

Tom sighed and rubbed long fingers over his aching temples. 'I wish someone had warned me.'

'Why?' Jack took a slug of beer. 'I thought you weren't interested in her anyway.'

Tom reached for his beer. He'd thought that, too.

But seeing her again had unsettled him more than he would have thought possible.

Being on the receiving end of her cool indifference had made him feel as though he'd lost something special.

At that moment the kitchen door flew open and Bryony stalked into the room, her whole manner confrontational.

Tom rose to his feet, his own gaze equally accusing. Ordinarily they were as close as a brother and sister could be, but tonight they glared at each other like enemies.

'Why didn't you tell me that she was coming back?' Tom's voice was hard and Bryony's gaze was equally hard as she met her brother's eyes.

'And good evening to you, too, Tom.' She leaned forward and kissed Jack, her expression softening slightly. Then she straightened and shrugged out of her wool coat.

'You should have told me she was coming back,' Tom snarled, and Bryony lifted an eyebrow, refusing to be intimidated by the dangerous light in her brother's eyes.

'Why? What reason did I have to believe you even cared? You ended it, remember?'

Colour touched Tom's cheekbones and his jaw tightened. 'That is none of your business.'

'It's my business when you expect me to help you smooth the path with her.'

'I can't change the past.' Tom sat back down in his chair and reached for his beer. 'And Sally and I need to move on. We can't do that if we don't have a conversation. We need to clear the air.'

'You mean you need to make yourself feel OK about what you did.'

Tom tensed, realizing with a considerable amount of discomfort that she was right. His conscience was troubling him. And he had a feeling that a conversation wasn't going to cure his problem.

'I did what I thought was right at the time.'

'Right for her or right for you?' Bryony put her hands on her hips, her expression disapproving, and Jack frowned.

'Bry, this really isn't our business.'

Bryony ignored him, her eyes still on her brother. 'You drove her away and now you're expecting her to be pleased to see you again.'

'I'm not expecting that.' Tom cursed softly and ran a hand over the back of his neck. 'And I didn't drive her away. She left.'

'Because of you! Because you didn't want her and she couldn't live in this small community alongside a man who'd rejected her. Do you know your problem?' Bryony glared at him. 'You just can't bear the fact that there's a woman in the world who doesn't think you're God's answer to romance. You broke Sally's heart but you want her to say, "That's fine, Tom." *Well, it isn't fine!*'

Tom's eyes narrowed. 'You're being emotional about this.'

Bryony gave a growl of feminine frustration. 'And you're being ice cold, as usual! Show a modicum of sensitivity here, Tom Hunter! You decided you didn't want her. End of story.'

It wasn't the end of the story.

Not by a long way.

It had been so much more complicated than that.

'You should have told me she was back.'

'Why would I do that? I assumed it would be of no interest to you.'

Tom gritted his teeth. 'Sally and I were together for almost three years, for goodness' sake. Of course I would have been interested in the fact that she was back.'

'You drove her away, so I assumed her return was a matter of the same indifference to you.'

Tom closed his eyes briefly and muttered something under his breath. 'Whose side are you on?'

'Sally's,' Bryony replied sweetly. 'And if you want my opinion, she should have blacked your eye seven years ago when she found you with that—that—*tart*!'

Jack winced. 'Sweetheart, you—'

'Don't *sweetheart* me!' Bryony glared at her husband. 'Tom behaved horribly to Sally.'

'I wasn't *with* anyone,' Tom gritted, 'I went on one date with another woman, that's all! One date and it was after Sally and I had split up. After we'd agreed to see other people.'

'*You'd* agreed to see other people,' Bryony reminded him coldly. 'Sally was so devastated she just sat in her flat broken into tiny pieces.'

Tom winced at the description. 'It was the wrong time for both of us and we were in an impossible situation, Bry, as you would realize if you took the emotion out of it and looked at it logically.'

'And if you took the logic out of it and looked at it emotionally, you might stand some chance of sustaining a relationship with a woman!' Bryony glared at him.

'You threw away something really special. You're as bad as Jack!'

'Hey!' Jack put a hand on his chest, totally affronted. 'I married you!'

Bryony breathed out heavily. 'Only because I told you some home truths,' she said bluntly. 'If I'd left it to you, you'd still be dating half of Cumbria. You were so afraid of emotional involvement I virtually had to tie you up and beat you before you'd agree that you loved me.'

Jack gave her a sexy wink. 'I'm not sure you should be revealing the details of our bedroom antics to your brother, darling.'

Bryony pulled a face. 'What I'm saying, as you well know, is that both of you have spent the best part of your adult lives avoiding commitment. Of course Sally doesn't want a conversation with you, Tom. Why would she? You lost that right when you started dating other people.'

Tom sighed. 'You make it sound like a crime, but we weren't together any more, Bry.'

'That's right.' Bryony's tone was chilly. 'You weren't. You left the rest of us to clear up the mess.'

'I tried to see her, to check that she was all right.'

'Well, of course she wasn't all right! And she didn't want your pity!'

Tom gritted his teeth and drew in a steadying breath. 'Do you realize how contradictory you're being?'

Jack groaned out a warning. 'For goodness' sake, don't tell her that.'

'Well, on the one hand she's telling me I left her to comfort Sally, and on the other she's telling me that Sally wouldn't have wanted me around anyway.'

Bryony scowled at him. 'You behaved badly!'

Jack yawned and reached for his beer. 'OK, honey,

give the guy a break. He's not the first person to have ended a relationship that wasn't working. I think we should all move on.'

'That is precisely what I'm trying to do,' Tom said harshly, 'only Sally won't give me the chance to discuss it. Perhaps I ought to tell her that she's allowed to black my eye if it will make her feel better.'

In fact, he half hoped she would. Perhaps it would ease his conscience.

Bryony plopped down on the chair next to Jack and gave a sigh. 'I don't think it matters what you promise,' she said wearily. 'You're not going to find it easy to get near her. She doesn't want to talk to you.'

And why was that?

Tom's eyes narrowed thoughtfully, his sharp brain clicking into action. Surely if Sally was as indifferent to him as she was pretending, then one conversation was hardly going to cause a problem. She could just listen and then walk away.

Unless she was afraid that the walking away would be hard.

Jack lifted his beer. 'Never was easy to get near to Sally Jenner. She always kept people at a distance.'

Except him. Tom frowned.

He was the one person who'd been allowed to get close to her.

'And can you blame her for that?' Bryony defended her friend quickly. 'She spent her childhood moving from foster-home to foster-home, with no security and no one she could trust or love.'

Tom shifted uncomfortably.

Sally had trusted him. And she'd loved him. *Until he'd betrayed that trust and thrown her love back in her face.*

'This is a small community,' he said finally, draining his beer and standing up. 'Sally and I need to clear the air if we're going to be able to work together. Are you going to tell me where she's living, Bry?'

Bryony kept her eyes on the table. 'I'm sorry, Tom. I can't.'

Tom cast an exasperated look at Jack who shrugged helplessly.

'Women.' He winked at his wife. 'Especially blonde women.'

Tom gritted his teeth, his sense of humour less in evidence. 'You know me well enough to know that I'll track her down sooner or later.'

Bryony looked at him. 'But it will have been without my help.'

'You're making things more difficult.'

'Difficult was what you did to her seven years ago,' Bryony said stiffly. 'Think about that while you're preparing your speech, big brother.'

Tom picked up his jacket and nodded to Jack. 'Thanks for the beer.'

'Any time,' Jack said mildly, ignoring his wife's glare. 'Any time. I have a feeling you're going to need it.'

By the time she arrived at work the next morning, Sally was back in control.

The first meeting was always going to be difficult, she assured herself, stuffing her bag into her locker and making her way onto the labour ward.

From now on it could only get easier.

Having made that assumption, it annoyed her intensely to find that her heart missed a beat when she saw

Tom walking towards her down the corridor with that loose-limbed stride that had always set her heart racing.

His eyes were tired and the roughness of his darkened jaw suggested that he'd been up for most of the night.

'Good morning.' He gave her a smile that made her catch her breath and she automatically shut down her feelings.

She didn't want to respond to that smile.

Didn't want to acknowledge the curl of awareness low in her pelvis.

'Busy night?'

'You could say that.' He gave a short laugh. 'Why don't babies keep regular hours?'

Sally shrugged, intending to pass him, but he caught her arm and pulled her close to him, his voice low and meant only for her.

'If Emma hadn't interrupted us, we would have had that conversation last night. How long do you think you can keep running, Sally?'

She drew breath, forcing herself to ignore the strength of his fingers on her arm. 'I'm not running, Tom.' She stepped neatly away from him, forcing him to release her. 'I'm walking. And we wouldn't have had a conversation. I don't want one.'

'Why? I'm offering you the opportunity to shout at me or black my eye.'

She gave a faint smile. 'Why would I want to do that?'

'Because I probably deserve it.'

She stilled. Was he apologizing? Was he admitting that he'd been wrong?

'You made the decision that was right for you, Tom.'

His jaw tightened. 'It was right for both of us.'

So he didn't think he'd been wrong.

He'd never regretted it.

A rush of emotion threatened to choke her but she held his gaze steadily and her voice was chilly. 'In that case, what is there to talk about?'

He sucked in a breath and looked uncertain, obviously thrown by her response. It occurred to her that it was the first time she'd ever seen Tom anything other than supremely confident. 'I just know I need to talk to you.'

Sally shook her head. 'There's nothing to be gained from rehashing the past. What happened, happened. It's done. You made the decision for both of us. I had no choice but to go along with that.'

Without waiting for his answer, she slid past him and carried on up the corridor without looking back, trying to control her heart rate.

She had no doubt that sooner or later he would force her into the conversation that he was obviously determined to have. But she was determined to postpone the moment for as long as possible.

'Good morning.' She smiled at Emma who was collecting a set of notes from the desk. One glance at the whiteboard told her that she was in for a busy day. 'Where do you want me?'

'Can you divide yourself into four?' Emma rolled her eyes. 'I've rung down to the ward to ask for some help up here. Everyone seems to have gone into labour at once.'

'Isn't that always the way?' Sally reached for the nearest set of notes. She didn't mind being busy. All she asked was that today's mother-to-be would have a normal delivery. She didn't think she could face another day working side by side with Tom.

'Perhaps you could take Charlotte Knight,' Emma said, staring at the board with her eyes narrowed. 'She's four centimetres dilated and she's asking for an epidural.

She seems to have made up her mind so I've put in a call to the anaesthetist.'

Sally nodded. 'You do a lot of epidurals here?'

'Not if we can help it.' Tom's deep, male voice came from behind them and Sally felt her heart miss a beat. She hadn't heard his approach. 'There is little doubt that epidurals are associated with longer labours, more use of oxytocin and more use of forceps and ventouse. We add in opiates and reduce the bupivacaine dose, which allows some mobility while maintaining adequate pain relief, but even so there is an increased rate of instrumental delivery. If we can encourage the mother to use a different sort of pain relief, we do.'

'Well, I failed with her, I'm afraid,' Emma said gloomily, spreading her hands in a gesture of resignation. 'I suppose it might be worth Sally giving it a try. You might have more luck.'

Sally tucked the notes under her arm and looked at Tom. 'I thought most obstetricians were more than happy to dive in with instruments. It's what you love doing.'

'Women are designed to give birth,' Tom said calmly. 'Given the right amount of support and encouragement and some patience on our part, most of them manage it extremely well by themselves.'

'Aren't you rather talking yourself out of a job?' Sally gave a faint smile and he shrugged.

'Believe it or not, I already have more than enough work to keep me from my bed at night.' He nodded to Emma. 'And on that note, I'm off to do a ward round then I'm going to bed, if I can remember where it is. It's so long since I last saw it that I may have trouble remembering, and I'm supposed to be working again tonight so there's not much hope of seeing it then either. You can call me if you need me.'

He strode off, leaving Emma staring after him wistfully. 'You see what I mean? Other doctors grab a woman as soon as she steps onto the labour ward and before you know it she's had her waters broken, a drip up and she's being given oxytocin. Tom lets a woman get on with it. He's wonderful. And he doesn't let the hospital management bully him into pushing patients through as fast as possible. Tom always says that labour takes as long as it takes.' She gave Sally a sheepish smile. 'Sorry. You've probably guessed that I'd have his babies by now if he asked me.'

Sally felt a sharp flash of pain. *She would have had his babies, too.*

'Not that I seriously entertain any hopes in that direction,' Emma said lightly. 'Our Mr Hunter is a workaholic. No time for a serious relationship. Was he like that when you knew him?'

'Probably.' Sally's smile was noncommittal. 'It was a long time ago.'

Seven years, six weeks, three days and seven hours to be precise.

'Anyway…' Emma waved a hand towards one of the delivery rooms '…go and have a chat with Charlotte. See if you can persuade her to try something different.'

'Did you discuss the pool?'

'She wasn't keen.'

'Aromatherapy?'

Emma shook her head. 'She didn't seem the type, but by all means go ahead. Tom would love you for ever if you manage to talk her out of an epidural.'

Sally picked up the notes and walked down the corridor, trying not to remember that at one point in her life she'd truly believed that Tom's love *would* last for ever.

But she'd been wrong.

Pushing away painful memories, she opened the door to the delivery room and smiled at the woman on the bed.

'Charlotte?' She put the notes down on the side and walked across the room. 'I'm Sally. I'm your midwife.'

The young woman was clutching the edge of the bed and breathing rapidly. 'This is agony. I want an epidural.'

'That's not a problem,' Sally said immediately. 'We've called the anaesthetist, but while we're waiting for him I just want to try a few things with you to help you relax. You're very tense, Charlotte, and that will make the pain worse.'

She talked quietly to the woman, calming her down, and then she dimmed the lights slightly and settled her in one of the chairs.

'Do you like massage?'

The woman made a sound halfway between a laugh and a sob. 'I love it. But I can't afford it very often since I gave up work.'

Sally smiled and picked up one of her bottles of essential oils. 'Then you're in luck. I'm part of the service. I'm just going to do your neck and shoulders to try and relieve the tension. If you get a contraction and you want me to stop, let me know.'

She smoothed her hands over the woman's skin and Charlotte gave a moan of pleasure. 'That feels amazing.'

Sally carried on massaging her, feeling the young woman gradually relax.

As each contraction came she helped her breathe properly and gradually Charlotte became calmer.

'You're coping really well,' Sally said quietly. 'Are you sure you want that epidural?'

Charlotte opened her eyes. 'I don't think I can cope without it.'

'You are coping. You're coping really well. And there are other things that we can try as well.'

Charlotte stirred and looked at her husband, 'What do you think?'

He shook his head. 'It's up to you, love. Whatever you feel is best.'

'You don't have to decide now,' Sally said, her hands still stroking the woman's back. 'Why don't we just delay the anaesthetist for a bit and see how we get on?'

Charlotte gave a sigh and closed her eyes again. 'All right.'

Sally spent the rest of the afternoon with Charlotte, keeping her as relaxed as possible, encouraging her and helping her breathings. As the contractions grew stronger, she used different aromatherapy oils and soothing music and helped Charlotte to breathe the gas and air.

'I can't believe she isn't screaming for an epidural,' Emma muttered, when Sally nipped outside for a quick break. 'You're a miracle worker.'

'I'm not.' Sally downed a glass of water quickly, reluctant to leave Charlotte for too long. 'I think someone had just persuaded her that an epidural is the answer. I don't think she'd even considered other options.'

She went back to Charlotte and stayed there until early evening when she nipped out to take a phone call from Oliver Hunter, Tom and Bryony's brother, inviting her over that evening to meet his new fiancée.

'It's great that you're home, Sally. The whole gang is back together at last. Come and have supper,' he said easily, his tone as warm and friendly as ever. As if she hadn't been away for seven years with no contact.

Sally gave a soft smile as she held the phone. Oliver always had been the more friendly of the two brothers. Open and straightforward, where Tom was complex and brooding.

Why couldn't she have fallen for Oliver?

Life would have been so much more straightforward if she had.

'So will you come?'

Sally's hand tightened on the receiver. Was it really possible to pick up the strands of friendship as if she'd never dropped them?

Suddenly she felt awkward. Awkward that she'd abandoned them all. But it had been the only way. If she hadn't cut the ties, she never would have survived. 'I don't know what time I'll finish here…'

'Doesn't matter,' Oliver said immediately. 'Come over whenever. Bry and Jack are coming, and a few others. I'm trying to integrate my Helen into the community.'

Sally hesitated, wanting to know whether Tom would be there but not able to form the question.

To ask the question would make it look as though she cared.

And, anyway, hadn't he said that he was working?

'I'll be there,' she said quickly, not giving herself the chance to think about the invitation any further. It would be nice to go out. Nice to see Oliver again.

She went back to Charlotte and in virtually no time she was fully dilated and ready to push.

Sally called for Emma and together they quietly delivered the baby with the minimum of fuss and bother.

'Well done, Charlotte,' Sally said quietly as she

handed the baby to her very tired but very proud mother.
'You were amazing.'

'I can't thank you enough.' Charlotte gazed down at
her baby daughter and tears filled her eyes. 'And I did
it all by myself.'

'That's right.' Sally smiled. 'All by yourself.'

Emma sniffed. 'And that's the way it should be done.'

'Another long day.' Sally changed into her jeans and a
jumper the exact colour of her eyes, slammed her locker
shut and pocketed the key. 'See you tomorrow, Emma.'

She ran down the stairs to the bike rack at the back
of the unit and grabbed her mountain bike.

It was a cold, clear evening and she rode fast, chasing
away the pressures of the past few days, enjoying the
bite of winter air against her cheeks.

Oliver answered the door with a smile. 'Sally!' He
stepped forward and hugged her tightly. 'It is so good
to see you. We've missed you.'

Touched by the warm welcome, Sally hugged him
back. She'd missed her friends so much, but she hadn't
truly realized how much until she'd had the letter from
Bryony. Her thoughts about home had always been dom-
inated by Tom, and somehow along the way she'd forgotten just how many longstanding friendships she had
in this small community.

For a moment she closed her eyes and allowed herself
the rare treat of being held by someone, and then she
pulled away and reached up to kiss his cheek, handing
him the bottle of wine she'd brought with her.

'Congratulations. Bryony tells me you finally met
Miss Right. The women of Cumbria must be in mourn-
ing.'

Oliver grinned. 'The fells are littered with sobbing

females. Come and meet Helen. Everyone's in the kitchen.'

Sally followed him through to the kitchen, smiling at Jack and Bryony and sniffing appreciatively. 'Smells good, Oliver.'

A pretty blonde girl stepped forward, a smile on her face as she greeted Sally. 'I'm Helen and I'm very pleased to meet you.'

'Likewise.' Sally glanced between them. 'I'm really delighted for the two of you. I hear you met at Bryony's wedding two months ago?'

'That's right.' Oliver slipped an arm round Helen's shoulders and hugged her. 'We're getting married in two weeks' time and before you ask the obvious question, no, she isn't pregnant but if I have my way she will be soon.'

Helen gave a shocked gasp and gave Oliver a little push. 'Oliver, that's awful! You shouldn't say things like that in company!'

Her face was scarlet with embarrassment and Oliver cupped her face in his hands and kissed her gently.

'That depends on the company.' His tone was smug and his blue eyes twinkled. 'This lot have always known I want a hundred children so it's time we got started.'

Genuinely pleased that they were so happy, Sally managed a smile and tried to ignore the ache in her heart.

It would happen to her, she told herself firmly.

One day it would happen to her.

'Have a drink.' Oliver handed her a glass of wine and then tilted his head as the doorbell rang. 'Be an angel and get that for me, Sal, while I finish cooking.'

The years fell away.

Suddenly she was 'Sal' again, and it felt good. Comfortable and safe.

During her childhood, being with Bryony, Oliver and Tom had been the nearest she'd come to belonging anywhere.

The nearest she'd had to family.

Suddenly she was glad that Bryony had married Jack. If she hadn't, would she herself ever have found the courage to come home? Preoccupied, Sally walked to the front door and tugged it open, her smile of greeting fading as she found herself face to face with Tom.

CHAPTER FOUR

HE WAS dressed in black leathers, his motorbike helmet tucked under one arm, the dark stubble on his jaw an indication that he'd left the hospital in a hurry. He looked dark and dangerous and his blue gaze locked on hers in blatant challenge, his mouth tightening as their eyes met.

Her heart stumbled and her stomach lurched but her instinct to close the door and pretend that there was no one there was curbed by the knowledge that this wasn't her house. She had no right to shut him out of his brother's home.

And she really didn't want him to know that she cared that much.

It was the one thing that stopped her dropping her glass and reaching for her coat.

Pride.

She was no longer so weak and pathetic that she believed that she couldn't exist without Tom Hunter in her life.

Calling on inner reserves, she reminded herself that part of coming home had been to confront what she'd felt for Tom, and she couldn't do that by avoiding him.

Avoiding him implied that she still felt something for him, and she wasn't that foolish.

'Well?' A faint smile of self-mockery touched his firm mouth. 'Are you going to slam the door in my face?'

The fact that she'd considered doing exactly that brought a trace of colour to her cheeks and she stepped to one side to let him in, careful that her gaze revealed nothing.

'I hope I'm not that uncivilized, Tom.'

She wanted to ask why he wasn't working, but stayed silent. She didn't want him knowing that she cared that much or that she'd taken that much notice of what he'd told her earlier.

'I want to talk to you, Sally.' He unzipped his jacket and she flinched, her eyes drawn instinctively to his chest and then away, fixing on some point in Oliver's hallway.

She forced herself to resist the command in his tone. She'd been making her own decisions for years now and she intended to carry on doing so. To listen to what he had to say would risk being sucked back into the darkness from which she'd fought so hard to escape.

'There is absolutely nothing that you and I need to talk about, and this is supposed to be an evening spent with friends,' she replied calmly, turning away from him with as much dignity as she could muster. 'I haven't seen Oliver for years and I want to get to know Helen.'

Strong fingers caught her wrist and swung her back round to face him. 'And you and I no longer share the category of friends?'

She closed her eyes, breathing deeply.

Friends?

Once he'd been everything to her. Her friend, her lover—*her world.*

His fingers tightened and she felt his touch with every fibre of her being. Her traitorous body yearned for more. Yearned for everything this man was capable of giving.

And then she remembered that he wasn't capable of giving enough.

He hadn't been able to make that commitment to her.

And neither had anyone else in her life.

And she'd finally learned to live her life alone, depending on no one.

'Of course we can be friends.' Her answer was suitably bland. 'After all, we're working together.'

'That's colleagues,' he replied softly, his eyes narrowing slightly. 'Friendship is something completely different. We had it once.'

'And I seem to remember that you decided that you no longer valued that friendship.' She gave a cool smile to indicate that the conversation was over, ignoring the traitorous thump of her heart. 'Oliver is handing out drinks in the kitchen. If you don't want to miss out I suggest you move quickly.' With a determined twist of her wrist she freed herself and walked towards the kitchen with a determined stride, feeling his frustration with a faint flicker of satisfaction.

Not everything goes your way, Tom Hunter.

She walked back into the kitchen and said, 'Tom's here,' in her most casual voice, and then proceeded to top up her glass of wine.

There was a tense silence and Bryony put her hands on her hips and glared at Oliver. 'You invited *Tom*?'

'Why not?' Oliver's tone was calm. 'He's my brother. I refuse to stop socializing with him just because he used to go out with Sally. It's been seven years, for crying out loud. It's history. We all need to move on.'

'But—'

'Hush, Bry,' Sally said quietly, reaching out and squeezing her friend's shoulder to reassure her. 'Oliver's right. It's fine.'

And it *was* fine. She was totally in control.

She'd always known that she wouldn't be able to avoid Tom. And she didn't want to.

What she wanted was to work and live in a community alongside him and not feel anything.

Bryony rubbed her fingers over her temples, visibly stressed, and Oliver glanced towards the door where Tom was leaning, listening to the exchange in silence, his handsome face devoid of expression.

He'd removed his leathers to reveal a pair of snugly fitting jeans and a black jumper that simply accentuated his masculine looks.

He looked dark and dangerous and just about as sexy as it was possible for a man to be.

'I can't understand why you use the motorbike in winter.' Oliver's tone was mild. 'It's freezing out there and it worries Mum.'

'I've been worrying Mum since I was able to walk,' Tom drawled, strolling to the fridge and helping himself to a bottle of beer. 'And I like the fresh air. Good evening, Bryony.'

Ignoring the irony in his tone, Bryony glared at him and Oliver sighed.

'You're destroying the atmosphere of my dinner party,' he said mildly. 'Sort it out, bro, or we'll all get indigestion.'

'I intend to sort it out.' Tom pushed the fridge door shut, his eyes on Sally. 'So what do you say, Sally? Can we work together and socialize together without creating an atmosphere?'

Sally tensed, her fingers gripping the stem of her wineglass so tightly that it was in danger of snapping.

He stepped towards her, his gaze only for her. 'My sister thinks you should hit me. So do it, Sally.'

She felt smothered by his closeness, by his overwhelming masculinity. She took a deep breath and then wished she hadn't because his tantalizing male smell filled her head and clouded her senses. She had only to lift a hand to touch him but she kept both hands firmly by her sides and stared at the floor.

She decided to let him speak. If she let him speak then he'd leave her alone.

'I don't want to hit you.'

'You should. It would make Bryony feel better. And stop looking at the floor.' Tom lifted his hands and cupped her face, forcing her to look at him. 'I want you to look at me.'

Startled by his touch, she stood without moving, staring into her past, feeling the brush of his fingers on her sensitized skin.

She'd loved this man so much.

'I'm sorry, Sally.' His voice softened with genuine regret. 'Sorry for hurting you so badly.'

Those blue eyes drew her in and she struggled against the powerful sexual attraction that still existed between them.

With a monumental effort she broke the contact. First the emotional, then the physical.

Shutting herself down, she stepped backwards.

'You did what you believed was right,' she said lightly, managing what she hoped was a dignified smile. 'And it's in the past. Oliver's right—we've all moved on. The future is what's important now.'

And her future wasn't going to feature this man.

She would never allow herself to be so vulnerable to hurt and pain again.

She lifted her chin and looked at Oliver. 'When are we eating? I'm starving.'

There was a collective sigh of relief around the room and everyone started talking again.

Everyone except Tom.

His eyes were firmly fixed on Sally, his blue gaze narrow and assessing as he looked at her.

Instantly she turned away, determined not to allow him access to her thoughts.

He'd always been good at reading her.

Too good.

That amazing bond of understanding had been fundamental to the powerful chemistry they'd shared. And it had made it even harder when he'd ended the relationship.

People had come and gone from her life before, but none of them had understood her as Tom had, and it had made the loss even greater.

Determined to normalize the situation, she quickly involved Bryony in a discussion about her new role as a GP registrar.

'I've only been doing it for a month.' Bryony held out her glass so that Oliver could top it up. 'I'm just grateful I haven't got Oliver as my trainer. It would be only marginally worse than working with Jack.'

'Confronting perfection on a daily basis can be challenging,' Jack agreed sympathetically, his expression solemn as he looked at his wife.

'Don't start,' Bryony warned, glancing over her shoulder to the Aga. 'Something's about to boil over, Helen.'

Helen gave a gasp and dashed to retrieve the pan while Oliver laughed. 'OK, everybody out! We're distracting her. Table's laid in the conservatory. Helen and I will finish up here.'

He ushered them out of the kitchen while Helen drained the vegetables and removed the plates from the warmer.

Wishing she could have stayed in the relative safety of the kitchen, Sally walked into Oliver's huge glass conservatory and eyed the table warily. Bryony and Jack sat down together on one side of the table, still in mid-argument, which meant that, wherever she sat, she'd be near Tom.

She almost laughed. Of course she'd be near Tom. The table was laid for six. How could she not be near him? And with everyone else in couples, how could this not be intimate?

She was just contemplating whether it would be less nerve-racking to sit opposite him or next to him when Tom settled himself in a vacant chair and looked at his sister.

'So are you going to the training session tomorrow night?'

Relieved that she wasn't the focus of attention, Sally slipped into the seat next to Tom, deciding that at least that way she wouldn't have to look at him.

'Yes.' Bryony reached for a bread roll and broke it in half. 'So is Sally. Sean couldn't wait to get her back on the team.'

Oliver walked into the room, carrying a huge dish piled high with a delicious-smelling risotto. 'Didn't take him long to talk you into that, Sal.'

Sally took a plate from Helen with a smile of thanks. 'You know Sean.'

Helen spooned some risotto onto her plate. 'So you're a mountain girl, too?'

Oliver gave a snort. 'Sally is more of a mountain girl than any of us. She's been doing the serious stuff. And she's going to tell us all about it.' He topped up everyone's glasses and then raised his towards Sally. 'Cheers. And now we want to hear everything, down to the last gory detail.'

'Not much to tell.' She'd left in a mess and had somehow managed to rebuild her life. It wasn't a story she cared to tell in front of Tom. 'After I left here, I spent some time in the Himalayas. Climbing and working in a clinic there. It was good experience.'

'What did you climb?'

It was typical of Tom to want the detail. When they'd been young they'd exchanged details of every route.

'Well, not Everest,' she said lightly, 'although I spent some time at base camp and lower down the valley.' She hesitated. 'I joined an expedition climbing Ama Dablam, and that was amazing. Such a beautiful mountain.'

Tom's expression changed and he looked at her with a new respect. 'You climbed Ama Dablam? That's a serious climb. How did you cope with the altitude?'

'Surprisingly well.'

'Dad and I climbed it. It was our first real Himalayan experience.'

She looked at him and for a moment there were only the two of them in the room. 'I remember. You raved about it. It was one of the reasons I went there.'

Because going somewhere that he'd been had somehow maintained a link. And she didn't want to remember how desperately she'd needed that link. Anything that reminded her of Tom. Anywhere that Tom had been, as if he'd imprinted part of himself on the places that he'd visited.

Suddenly realizing that she'd revealed too much, she dropped her eyes to her plate. 'After Ama Dablam, I travelled. I met a friend and we went mountain biking around Nepal—that was great. We had a good time.'

'A *friend*?' Bryony's eyes teased her from across the table. 'We want to hear more about this *friend*.'

Everyone laughed except Tom, who gazed at her face in brooding silence.

'You went mountain biking in the Himalayas?' Helen looked at her in awe. 'You make me feel exhausted just thinking about it. Didn't you relax at all?'

Sally fiddled with her food and gave a half-smile. 'I find climbing relaxing.'

It required all her concentration and that left no room for other thoughts to intrude. Thoughts of Tom. She'd run so that the pain couldn't catch her and she'd continued to run until she'd finally been sure that she'd left the worst of the agony behind.

'Well, it certainly doesn't sound relaxing to me.' Helen gave a little shudder and Oliver laughed and took her hand.

'My wife is a townie at heart,' he teased gently, 'but we're trying to convert her. If she doesn't wear high heels for a few days she has serious withdrawal symptoms.'

Helen's eyes mocked him. 'You're always so derogatory about my choice of footwear, but I don't hear you complaining when we go out.'

'I admit it.' Oliver grinned at her. 'My fatal weakness. A woman in high heels.'

'Enough of your strange fetishes.' Bryony frowned at her brother and turned back to Sally. 'I had your letter from the Karakorum.'

Helen looked confused. 'Where—or what—is the Karakorum?'

Tom stirred. 'It's a range of mountains in Pakistan.' He looked at Sally. 'You went to K2?'

'I worked as base camp manager for one of the expeditions,' she told him, 'and in one of the clinics there.

And when that finished one of them persuaded me to travel to Australia so I did and I got a job as a midwife.'

The conversation switched to obstetrics and Sally concentrated on her meal, wondering why she couldn't relax.

She'd grown up with these people. They were the closest thing to family she had, and yet the only person she was aware of was Tom.

Despite the fact that his chair was several inches from hers, she was supremely conscious of him. The hard muscle of his thigh was tantalizingly close to hers and suddenly she wished she could flick a switch in her body that would delete for ever her awareness of this man.

And he was tense.

She could feel it.

He lounged in his chair, listening to the conversation, his long fingers tapping the table.

'All right, pay attention. We have some news.' Bryony tucked her hand into Jack's and beamed at everyone.

Sally looked at her friend with interest, glad of a distraction from Tom. 'What news?'

'I'm pregnant.' Bryony spoke softly, her gaze slightly shy as she looked at Jack. 'Two months gone. Not very much really, so we haven't told anyone except Mum. And now you.'

Helen gave a squeal of delight and dashed round the table to hug Bryony. Oliver shot Jack an amused glance.

'No need to ask what you were doing on your honeymoon. Congratulations.'

'Yes, congratulations.' Genuinely pleased for her friend, Sally smiled across the table. 'It looks as though I came home at the right time. I've got seven months to get used to the idea of answering to "Aunty Sally".'

Tom's gaze was fixed on her face. 'Why did you decide to come home?'

Sally reached for her wine, her hand perfectly steady. 'Because it was time,' she said softly, still smiling at Bryony. 'I realized I was missing out on the lives of people who matter to me.'

Bryony looked at Tom. 'I want you to deliver me.'

Tom frowned and his fingers stilled. 'That would not be a good idea, and you know it.'

'You delivered Ellie MacAllister.' Bryony's gaze softened as she looked at her brother. 'You saved her life.'

'Ellie is not my sister.'

'But she's a close friend.'

Tom let out a long breath. 'That's different.'

'I don't see why your sister should be deserving of less than a friend. There's no one else I trust,' Bryony confessed quietly, and Tom sighed.

'Bry, I can't.' He took a slug of wine and stared broodily at his glass. 'I'll have a word with Chris Knight. He seems pretty good to me.'

'Pretty good isn't good enough,' Bryony said tartly, and Jack grinned.

'"Pretty good" is high praise from your brother, you should know that. The guy's obviously a genius.'

Tom gave a wry smile. 'He seems solid enough and we think along the same lines.'

'I want *you*,' Bryony said stubbornly, and Tom's gaze shifted to Jack.

'Don't look at me,' Jack muttered. 'When Bry gets something stuck in her head, there's no shifting it. You should know that.'

Tom was silent for a few moments and then he looked at his sister. 'I promise to be there when you deliver, but I'm not being responsible for the actual delivery.'

Bryony hesitated. 'You'll be there? You'll intervene if you see them doing something wrong?'

'People don't do things wrong in my department.' Tom ran a hand over the back of his neck. 'And, yes, I'll be there.'

Bryony smiled at him, warmth and gratitude in her eyes. 'Thanks, Tom.'

Sally was suddenly aware that he was studying her again and she felt the tension rise inside her.

Why had he asked her that question about her reasons for coming home?

Had he expected a declaration of undying love?

If so then he was doomed to disappointment.

She stood up, suddenly needing to be in her own.

'I'd better go. I'm on an early tomorrow.' She glanced at her watch and then smiled at Helen. 'It was a wonderful meal and a lovely evening. Thank you so much for inviting me.'

'Come again soon.' Helen glanced at Jack and Bryony. 'Are you giving Sally a lift home? She can't possibly ride her bike this late.'

'You're talking to a girl who mountain biked around the Himalayas,' Oliver said dryly, his eyes amused as he looked at his fiancée. 'I don't suppose anyone looked out for her then.'

'Well, that doesn't mean we shouldn't look out for her now,' Helen said firmly, 'and she isn't riding that bike of hers home this late at night.'

Something shifted inside Sally and she felt an instant bond with Helen.

She was an incredibly kind person.

'Thank you,' she said gruffly, 'but I'll be fine, really.'

'Helen's right, you shouldn't cycle this late. I'll give

you a lift.' Tom rose to his feet and lifted an eyebrow in her direction, challenging her to refuse.

She lifted an eyebrow. 'You're on a bike, too, remember?'

Tom's eyes gleamed with amusement. 'Not the same thing, as you well know.'

Sally glanced down at herself. 'I'm hardly dressed for a ride on a motorbike in freezing March.'

'I've got a spare helmet and you can borrow a set of leathers from here,' Tom said easily. 'Oliver?'

'We'll take her,' Bryony interrupted quickly, her expression troubled as she looked at Sally. 'She doesn't want to go on the back of your motorbike. It's a totally uncivilized mode of transport.'

'Sally isn't like you,' Tom said softly, his blue eyes fixed firmly on Sally. 'She used to love my motorbike. I can't believe she's really changed that much.'

Sally stared at him, hardly able to breathe. Why did she have the feeling that this conversation wasn't about motorbikes? It was about the person she used to be.

But she wasn't that person any more.

She wasn't the same girl who had been so crazy about Tom that all the other parts of her life had blurred into insignificance.

Bryony reached for her keys. 'I'm taking her home,' she said firmly, and Oliver sighed.

'Well, in that case you'll have to come back here afterwards, because Jack and I have got things to discuss.'

'Thanks, Bry, but I'll go with Tom.' The last thing Sally wanted was to put Bryony to so much trouble when she'd already been so generous in every way. It was just one short motorbike ride. How could that be a problem? And it was hardly intimate. They wouldn't even be able to have a conversation and he couldn't see her face once they were on the bike. It would be fine.

She looked at the leathers that Oliver was holding out to her, her eyes suddenly wary as she recognized them. 'They're mine...'

'You gave them to us when you left. Naturally, we hung onto them.'

Sally stood for a moment, remembering the time she'd bought the leathers. The same time she'd thought she'd be with Tom for ever.

Putting them on would be like going back in time, and that was the last thing she wanted to do.

Then she felt Tom's eyes on her and reached for the leathers. 'Thanks.'

She wriggled into them, took the helmet from Tom and said her goodbyes, by which time Tom was already seated on the motorbike, his black helmet concealing his features and giving him an air of menace and danger.

Sally swallowed, suddenly realizing what she'd committed herself to. Why on earth hadn't she just agreed when Bryony had offered to drive her home? It would have been the safe option.

But she'd never chosen the safe option in her life and Bryony had already done more than enough.

She looked at his powerful figure straddling the bike with careless ease and suddenly her body throbbed in an instinctive and totally feminine response to the macho figure he presented. But his sexual magnetism had never been in question, she reasoned, hating herself for the strength of her reaction. That was why she'd made such a fool of herself over him in her teens.

Looking at the space on the back of his bike, she felt her breath catch.

How could she have thought that riding on a bike with

him would be less intimate than travelling in a car? It was so much more intimate. On a bike she would be wrapped around him, her body locked against his as it had been so many times in the past.

'Are you coming?' His deep voice was molten male invitation and she was suddenly thankful that the helmet concealed her expression.

'Yes.'

Comforting herself that the journey was relatively short, she stepped up to the bike and swung her leg over, sitting as far back in the saddle as possible, trying to keep her distance.

Without speaking, he reached back and found her arms, lifting them and wrapping them around him, forcing her to draw close, to slot her body against his.

She felt the warmth and strength of him pressed against her, felt the powerful play of male muscle against hers as he steered the bike out of Oliver's drive.

As they picked up speed she felt the familiar kick of excitement and closed her eyes, transported back in time.

It was a mistake. Like an addict who allows himself just one more taste of a dangerous substance, she felt the insidious pull of desire. A need that couldn't be controlled by common sense. Feeling the traitorous warmth spread through her body, she wondered despairingly how it was that you could know something was bad for you and yet still want it so badly.

Other men, she told herself firmly.

There were other men out there and she was going to meet one of them...

She was so preoccupied by her own internal battle that it wasn't until Tom approached Bryony's cottage that she realized that she hadn't even told him where she lived.

The bike slowed and she pulled herself back from the edge of insanity, sliding off the back of the bike before he'd even brought it to a halt.

She dragged off the helmet and handed it to him, shaking her blonde hair in an automatic gesture.

'So how did you know where I was living?'

'A simple matter of deduction,' he drawled. 'My little sister seems to have given herself the role of protector and her cottage is empty. It would be a logical decision to offer it to you.'

'I'm finding myself somewhere of my own soon.'

He shrugged. 'Why bother? This cottage is great and it's not that far from the hospital.'

Because after seven years of travelling she was ready to have somewhere that was her own. Even if all she could afford was something tiny.

It would be all hers.

But she had no intention of sharing those thoughts with Tom.

'Goodnight. Thanks for the lift.'

'Are you going to invite me in?' His voice was velvety dark and tempting and she stared at him like a rabbit caught in headlights, the physical pull of his presence as powerful as ever.

'Why would I?'

'Because, whatever you might say to the contrary,' he drawled softly, 'you know you want to. All evening you felt me next to you in the same way that I felt you. This thing between us hasn't gone away, Sally.'

Her insides lurched alarmingly and she backed away a few steps. 'What I know,' she said coldly, 'is that you are as arrogant as ever.'

But despite her accusation she could feel the insidious

warmth spread through her veins, fuelled by the lazy, confident look in his blue eyes.

When she'd been younger, it had been one of the many things that had attracted her to him. His unshakable self-confidence, his nerve and courage in confronting the world, his total belief in his ability to conquer all. For someone as insecure as her, he'd represented security. She'd always believed that nothing would ever go wrong as long as Tom was there.

But the thing that had gone wrong had been Tom himself.

Like everyone else in her life, eventually he'd pushed her away.

'So are you inviting me in?' He sat easily on the bike, watching her, totally relaxed. Or was he? His blue eyes were sharp and alert and fixed on her face, reading her every reaction with lethal accuracy.

'No, Tom. I'm not. Thanks for the lift.' She delved in her bag for her keys and turned to walk down the path to the cottage, but his arm snaked out and strong fingers closed over her arm, preventing her escape.

'You can deny it as much as you like, but it's still there.'

She stood still, trapped by the strength of his fingers and the truth in his words.

It *was* still there.

And that made it doubly difficult to do what she had to do.

But it didn't make it impossible.

'Goodnight, Tom.' With a determined effort and more willpower than she'd known she possessed, she pulled away from him for the second time that evening and walked down the path without looking back.

* * *

Tom rode the motorbike home at a pace that would have horrified his mother, but even the sudden burst of death-defying speed and power didn't relieve the throbbing tension that had built within him during the evening.

He locked the bike away and let himself into his house, contemplating the undeniable fact that, of all the women he'd been with in his life, Sally Jenner was the only one who had ever held his attention.

But she'd wanted a level of commitment that had unsettled him.

She'd been young and mixed up. Shifted from foster-home to foster-home, searching for security and acceptance. And unconditional love. Someone who wouldn't push her away when the going got tough.

And hadn't he done just that?

He cursed softly, reminding himself that he'd been in an impossible situation.

Sally had been so lonely and unloved that she'd treated him like a lifeline, and he'd known that the only way she was ever going to find confidence, find her place in the world, would be if they parted company. He'd been mature enough to realize how desperate she'd been for some sort of stability in her life, and he'd been afraid that her love for him had been fuelled by a desperation for security.

And looking at her this evening, looking at that poise and confidence, he could almost convince himself that he'd done the right thing.

But then he'd felt the pulsing, throbbing tension between them, and the question came back to taunt him as it had a million times over the last seven years.

What if he hadn't ended it?

Wondering why life was so damn complicated, Tom tugged open the fridge to retrieve another beer when he remembered that he'd already had one and it was still possible that he'd be called back to the hospital.

So instead he made himself a coffee and took it into his huge living room.

He sprawled on one of the leather sofas, staring blindly, thinking about the one woman who was never far from his mind.

When she'd chosen to leave Cumbria he'd been relieved. He had been fully aware that living in the same community as Sally Jenner and not wanting to ravish her twenty-four hours a day had been more than his willpower would have been able to cope with.

Even believing that his decision had been right for both of them, it hadn't made it any easier to live with.

He'd hurt her. Badly. Which had reduced him from friend and lover to just another person who'd rejected her.

What he hadn't anticipated was that seven years of separation wouldn't dull his desire for her in even the smallest degree.

All that the time had done had been to increase his doubt.

He stirred slightly, his gaze sliding around the stylish room that he'd designed himself, noticing how empty it was. Usually he found comfort in returning to the peace and order of his home.

But tonight something had changed.

Tonight his house didn't feel peaceful, it felt silent.

It didn't feel private, it felt lonely.

Suddenly he'd found himself wishing that he shared it with a woman, but not just any woman.

Sally.

The connection between them was as powerful as ever, even though she was choosing to deny it.

And who could blame her for that?

Suddenly he wished it were Sally who was pregnant, *with his child*.

Shocked by his thoughts, he rose to his feet and paced the generous expanse of his living room, wondering just what on earth was happening to him.

Sally dragged herself through the next few days at work, feeling totally exhausted. The strain of working in such close proximity to Tom was affecting her sleep pattern and she was permanently tired.

And she was thinking too much.

Thinking about the past.

Gritting her teeth and promising herself that she'd spend the weekend outdoors, she walked onto the unit for her last shift before her days off, frowning slightly as her mountain rescue team pager bleeped.

Moments later Tom strode onto the unit, his expression urgent.

'Grab your things, we need to get going.'

'Going?' Sally looked at him, her hand still on her pager. 'Surely we can't both leave the unit?'

Emma gave her a little push. 'We're quiet, and anyway Chris is around and I can get some help from the ward if I need it. What's happening, Tom?'

'Would you believe me if I told you that Lucy Thomas has called from somewhere in the Langdales? She's fallen and hurt her ankle.'

'Lucy?' Emma gaped at him. 'But she must be eight months pregnant by now!'

'Apparently she felt like some fresh air.' Tom let out a breath. 'I have to admit that of all the incidents I've ever attended, this one looks as though it might take the prize. It seems she fell and twisted her ankle and her husband can't move her. But we can talk about it on the way. I need to grab some extra equipment, Emma. Just in case.'

Sally frowned. 'But I thought it was her ankle that was injured.'

'It is, so far...' Tom was already striding down the corridor towards the storeroom, 'but I have a bad feeling about this one and clearly so does Sean. It's the reason he's asked for both of us to be there.'

He was back minutes later, stuffing various packages into a bag. In the meantime Sally had grabbed her coat and bag.

'You'll be pleased to hear I brought the four-wheel-drive today,' he said dryly, his eyes faintly mocking as he looked at her. 'So at least you'll be travelling in comfort.'

The hospital was only minutes from the base, and as soon as Tom pulled up in the car park Sally was out of the door and sprinting inside, grabbing her gear and changing quickly.

'I'm still waiting for the others,' Sean told them, ushering them across to the large map that was permanently displayed on the wall. 'She used a mobile phone but the battery went dead before she could be precise about their location. They stayed on the flat and she said they'd walked for about an hour. Given that she's eight months pregnant, that can't put them any further than here...' He stabbed the map with the end of his pen and frowned thoughtfully. 'We should be able to land a helicopter there if we have to.'

Tom shook his head in disbelief. 'What is a heavily pregnant woman doing, walking in the Langdales in this weather? Has the world gone mad?'

Sean grinned. 'It's a sunny day. Perhaps she wanted to deliver alfresco.'

'Don't even joke about it,' Tom growled, and Sally glanced at her watch.

'Let's get going.'

Part of her was quaking at the thought of going on alone with Tom, but part of her was relieved to be paired with him.

He was a highly skilled climber and a brilliant doctor. He was the perfect partner on any mountain rescue.

She just wished he wasn't so dangerously attractive.

Or, at the very least, she wished she no longer noticed or cared.

They both jumped back into the four-wheel-drive and Tom drove quickly to the point that he and Sean had identified from the map as being the closest to the path the couple seemed to have taken.

As she slipped her arms into her rucksack, Sally gave a shiver and looked up at the sky.

'The weather's closing in.'

'Of course it is.' Tom's tone was loaded with irony. 'You didn't really think you were going to carry out this rescue in sunshine, did you?'

Sally laughed. 'I would have hated it if we had. I love wild weather.'

He stilled, a strange expression flickering in his eyes as he looked at her. 'That's right.' His tone was suddenly soft. 'So you do.'

For a moment their eyes held and then she turned on her heel and started up the path, her emotions churning.

Being out in the mountains with him was the most bitter-sweet reminder of what they'd once shared. When they hadn't been working, they'd spent their whole lives outdoors. And she'd often chosen to climb when the weather had been at its worst, and Tom had always come with her.

Reminding herself that dwelling on the past just made the present harder to cope with, Sally increased her pace and strode confidently along the path that led along the valley floor, looking and listening and keeping a sharp eye on the weather. But all the time she was aware of Tom close behind her.

When she reached a fork in the path she paused, and Tom walked up to her, squinting up at the sky.

'It's not looking good. So which way? Left or right?'

Sally thought for a moment. 'Left,' she said decisively. 'And if they only walked for an hour, they shouldn't be far from here.'

She set off again and this time Tom walked by her side, adjusting his stride to hers. 'Why did you decide on left?'

'Instinct.' Sally glanced at him. 'If I was pregnant I would have taken this path. The views are better and it stays in the valley. The other one creeps up the mountain. It's steeper.'

'I can't imagine that would bother you,' Tom said dryly. 'I have no doubt that you'll still be climbing rock-faces when you're nine months pregnant.'

Sally dragged her eyes away from his.

She didn't want him to know how much she still longed for a child. It was one of the factors that had triggered their break-up. She'd wanted a baby and he'd thought she'd been too young.

She focused on the path. 'I see them. There—by that boulder.'

She increased her pace and they reached the couple quickly.

'Thank goodness you're here.' The man looked pale

and tired, his arm around his pregnant wife, who was lying on the ground, her bump smothered by an enormous weatherproof jacket. 'I didn't know what to do.'

'Well, first we need to sit her up,' Sally said quickly, shrugging the pack off her back and dropping to her knees next to the woman. 'I'm Sally. I presume you must be Lucy, unless there's another pregnant woman wandering the fells today.'

Tom dropped to his haunches. 'Lucy, what on earth do you think you're doing?'

The young woman gave a gasp and pressed a hand to her swollen abdomen. 'Oh, Mr Hunter! I didn't know that you'd come. I just fancied stretching my legs and we lost track of time and then I fell... I'm so sorry to be a nuisance. I can't believe I was stupid enough to slip!'

'You're not a nuisance,' Sally said immediately, 'but we do need to sit you up. Lying flat can cause problems at your stage of pregnancy because the weight of the baby presses on your major blood vessels.'

Tom was by her side and together they lifted the woman into a sitting position, propped against a large boulder.

'She's been having pains for the past half an hour,' Lucy's husband told them, his face drawn and anxious. 'We never should have come on this walk but it was such a beautiful day when we started out.'

Lucy screwed up her face and sucked in a breath. 'Oh—the pain is terrible.'

Tom frowned. 'In your ankle?'

'No.' Lucy shook her head, her eyes tightly shut as she struggled with the pain. 'I think the baby is coming.'

'Don't be ridiculous, Luce.' Her husband spoke in a falsely cheerful tone that was supposed to hide his anxiety and didn't. 'It isn't due for another three weeks and babies don't come that quickly.'

Lucy's features relaxed and she opened her eyes. 'Sorry to scare you, Mick, but it feels as though it's coming to me.'

Her husband glanced at Tom, horrified. 'She's wrong, isn't she? It can't possibly be coming here. That quickly.'

'Babies don't usually care too much about the venue and they don't always care about the timing either,' Tom said, squatting down beside Lucy and sliding a hand over her abdomen. 'They come when they're ready. And you're definitely having contractions. Sally, you monitor them. I'm going to take a look at your ankle, Lucy, so that we know what we're dealing with here. If you are in labour, we need to get you to hospital.'

Mick looked horrified. 'But it usually takes a long time, yes? Labour takes ages.'

'Usually, but not always,' Sally muttered, placing her hand on the top of Lucy's uterus to feel the strength of the contraction while Tom gently removed Lucy's boot. 'Has everything been normal in your pregnancy?' A gust of wind blew her blonde hair across her face and she anchored it back with her hand, contemplating the fact that she'd never had to ask these questions on a mountain rescue before. 'Any problems at all with you or the baby?'

Lucy shook her head. 'The baby was breech for a while but it turned about a month ago and the head has been engaged for a week. I saw Mr Hunter in clinic last week and he said everything was looking fine. Oh—' She broke off with a gasp of pain and Sally felt the power of the contraction as the uterus tightened under her hand.

'All right, Lucy, remember your breathing.' She glanced at her watch. 'Your contractions are very frequent. How long have you been in labour? When did the pains start?'

Lucy screwed up her face and shook her head. 'I didn't know I was in labour, but I was very uncomfortable in the car. We'd been to see my mum and we thought we'd stop and stretch our legs.'

'Stretch your legs?' Tom glanced up from examining her ankle. 'You walked for an hour.'

'It was just so beautiful we sort of lost track of the time, and walking helped the pain,' Lucy muttered. 'And it isn't as if pregnancy is an illness. I felt fine until I lost my balance.'

Tom looked at Sally, a question in his eyes. 'Well?'

'She's definitely in strong labour,' Sally said quietly, and Tom let out a breath.

'All right—let's take this one stage at a time,' he suggested, his tone calm as he finished his examination. 'In my opinion your ankle is sprained, not broken, but you're certainly not going to be walking anywhere on it for a while. If you're in labour, we need to get you to a hospital as fast as possible.'

'You can get a helicopter, yes?' Mick raked a shaking hand through his windblown hair, visibly shaken by the news that his wife was certainly in labour. 'Something fast.'

Lucy screwed up her face and grabbed Sally's hand. 'I've got another pain coming… Oh! I want to push—I can feel it.'

Even Tom looked startled by her terrified announcement and Sally found herself struggling not to smile, despite the potential seriousness of the situation. She'd never seen Tom out of his depth before, but at the moment he looked seriously disconcerted.

'I think you'd better unpack some of that equipment you brought, Tom,' she suggested calmly. 'It looks as though we're going to need it.'

Sally waited until the contraction had passed and then gently released Lucy's hand so that she could assess the progress of her labour more accurately. 'All right, I'm going to unzip your coat and see what's going on.'

Tom had moved to one side and was using the radio, presumably to talk to Sean at the mountain rescue base.

Sally concentrated on the labouring woman. Because there was no doubt in her mind that the woman was about to deliver. She didn't even need to pull on a pair of gloves and examine her. As Lucy was gripped by another powerful contraction, Sally clearly saw the top of the baby's head.

For a moment she felt a shaft of panic and then she reminded herself that there was no reason why a healthy woman couldn't deliver perfectly well outdoors. She had to forget about all the potential complications and concentrate on the job in hand. Their biggest problem was just the cold.

'Your baby is definitely coming, Lucy,' she said calmly, wishing Tom would get off the radio and help. Deciding that she'd better get on with it on her own, she delved into the rucksack and removed various packs. 'Mick, can you get a tent up, please? Something to keep the wind off. Check in Tom's rucksack.'

Creating a shelter wouldn't help that much, but at least it would be better than nothing.

Tom finished talking on the radio and strode back to her. 'They're sending a helicopter.'

Sally looked at him. 'You can't deliver a baby in a

helicopter,' she pointed out logically, and he ran a hand over the back of his neck.

'She's that close? Seriously?'

'I can see the head.' Sally looked at him, wondering what was the matter with him. 'I need a tent, Tom. Now. It's not much in the way of shelter, but it will help.'

Tom seemed to stir himself. 'Right. A tent. Mick, I need a hand.'

Sally left the two of them to sort out some shelter and turned her attention back to Lucy.

'Don't you worry about a thing,' she said cheerfully. 'We girls are going to manage this with no problem.'

Lucy gave a hysterical laugh and caught Sally's hand again. 'Would you believe that I actually dismissed the idea of a home birth because they convinced me it was dangerous for my first baby? And here I am on the side of a mountain! I can't believe this is happening!'

'Well, look on the bright side, at least you didn't climb up the mountain,' Sally said practically. 'And home birth is not dangerous in the right circumstances. Everything seems fine to me. The only thing we really need to worry about is the cold.'

'Have you delivered babies at home before?'

'I worked in Nepal for a while,' Sally told her chattily, happy to distract her. 'Hardly any of the women there make it to health centres of any sort, and plenty of other cultures think that home is the place to give birth. I once looked after a woman who insisted on giving birth in her garden, surrounded by candles.'

Lucy gave a hysterical laugh. 'But none of them chose to deliver in a howling gale on a mountainside.'

'You've certainly picked the best view,' Sally agreed with a laugh, grabbing the Pinard stethoscope from the rucksack and pressing it against Lucy's abdomen. 'This might be asking a bit much, but I want to try and listen to the baby's heart.'

For a few moments all she could hear was the wind and Lucy's gasps, and then she shifted the stethoscope slightly and there it was. The wonderfully reassuring gallop of the baby's heart.

'That's fine, Lucy.' She straightened. 'He or she seems to be perfectly happy. Obviously enjoying being outdoors.'

By now Lucy was inside the tent and she and Tom had manoeuvred a sterile sheet underneath her.

Lucy gave a low moan. 'I'm so scared. This isn't how it should be…'

'There's nothing to be scared of,' Sally said immediately. 'You're doing beautifully. Are you warm enough?'

Lucy nodded. 'I am, but what about the baby?'

'Well, at the moment he's still inside you so he's fine,' Sally said. 'We'll worry about his temperature once he's safely out.'

'You keep calling the baby he,' Lucy gasped, and Sally smiled, aware of Tom by her side.

'It's a boy. Definitely.' Her tone was dry. 'Only a man could cause this much trouble.'

Despite the tension of the situation, Lucy giggled. Tom picked up the banter. 'You're going to find out just what trouble is when this is over, Sally Jenner,' he threatened, his blue eyes gleaming as they locked on hers.

But despite his mockery and the kick of her heart, Sally couldn't be anything but glad that he was there.

She knew that if Lucy got into trouble, she was going to need him.

Lucy chuckled and then groaned. 'Don't make me laugh—it hurts. How can you be so relaxed?'

'Because there is absolutely nothing to be tense about,' Sally replied immediately. 'Childbirth is perfectly natural.'

Lucy grimaced. 'Until something goes wrong.'

'That's my line,' Tom muttered. He glanced at Sally and she rolled her eyes.

'Don't get all pessimistic on me, please, or I'll send the pair of you home and do this by myself.' She opened another pack and looked at Tom again. 'Could you draw up some Syntometrine? If you and Lucy are just going to sit there, panicking, I'll have to give the orders.'

He lifted a hand to show her that he'd already done it and it occurred to her that, despite everything that had happened, they were still a good team.

Lucy gave a gasp and shifted onto all fours. 'It's coming… I can feel it…'

Sally snapped on a new pair of gloves and glanced over her shoulder at Tom. 'We're going to need all the layers you can find, and I want a space blanket, too. OK, Lucy, the head is crowning. I want you to stop pushing if you can. That's it, good girl. Pant now, pant—that's it. Great.'

She used her left hand to control the escape of the head and reduce the chances of perineal tearing. As the baby's head was delivered she allowed it to extend and quickly checked that the cord wasn't around its neck.

'Fantastic, Lucy,' she said, glancing at Tom to check that he was ready to give the injection with the delivery of the anterior shoulder.

She saw the tension in his broad shoulders, the lines of strain around his eyes.

He was waiting for something to go wrong.

'Everything's fine,' she said quietly, as much for Tom's benefit as Lucy's. 'It's fine. And this is much the nicest delivery I've ever done. All we have to do is keep this baby warm once it's born.'

She could see that Lucy's body was doing everything it was supposed to do and there was no real reason why there should be problems. Their biggest problem was going to be keeping the baby warm once it was born.

Somewhere in the background she could hear the clack-clack of a helicopter, but she ignored it, waiting instead for the contraction that would finish the delivery of the baby.

Lucy screwed up her face and pushed again. Sally delivered the shoulders and finally the baby shot into her arms, yelling and bawling.

'Brilliant, Lucy! You clever girl!' Sally's eyes filled and she quickly blinked back the tears. 'You have a little boy.'

Tom immediately cleared the baby's airway and together they clamped the cord and then placed the child against Lucy's breast, wrapping mother and child up together.

Lucy gave a sob of disbelief. 'Is he all right?'

'He seems fine, but obviously we need to keep him warm and get him to hospital as fast as possible. As soon as your placenta is delivered and you're able to move, we're going to load you into that helicopter.'

Sally slid a hand over the top of Lucy's uterus, checking that it was contracting, and moments later the placenta was delivered.

She examined it closely and looked at Tom. 'It seems intact to me, but we need to take it to the hospital with us.'

He nodded. 'I'll talk to the helicopter crew about how we're going to do this.'

Satisfied that Lucy's uterus was contracting nicely and that she didn't seem to be losing more blood than was normal, Sally turned her attention to the baby, showing Lucy how to latch him onto the breast.

'Feeding will help your uterus contract and it will warm the baby up,' she explained, smiling as the little boy clamped his jaws around the nipple and started to suck. 'No problems there. He obviously has a natural ability. I told you he was a boy!'

Lucy looked at her, tears in her eyes. 'I can't thank you enough. You were amazing.'

'It was wonderful,' Sally said honestly, glancing over her shoulder as Tom stuck his head into the tent. 'Are we ready? The baby's feeding.'

'Great.' He smiled at Lucy. 'When you're ready to move we'll get you to the helicopter and take you to hospital. It's a very short hop.'

Tom stood in the doorway of the side ward, watching as Sally helped Lucy latch the baby onto the breast.

'He really is a natural,' she murmured, a satisfied smile on her face as the baby started to suck. 'And now you're both safe and sound.'

She was still dressed in her mountain rescue gear, her fair hair tangled from the wind and the drama, her cheeks flushed from the warmth of the room.

Tom felt something shift inside him.

She'd been fantastic.

She'd treated every moment of what could have been an obstetric nightmare as if it had been totally normal and wonderfully exciting. As if she'd delivered hundreds of babies outside on a freezing March day.

And she'd been in control every inch of the way.

She'd been the one to give him instructions, acting quickly and competently as soon as she'd realized that the baby had been coming.

He was more than impressed. He was amazed.

At that moment Lucy glanced up and saw him. 'Mr Hunter!'

'You look comfortable.' He walked into the room and Lucy smiled down at the nursing baby.

'I am comfortable. And relieved. Thank you so much, both of you.'

Tom smiled. 'I'd like to say that it's all in a day's work, but I'd be lying.' He ran a hand over the back of his neck and let out a breath. 'Next time go for a walk in a town. And make it a short one.'

Lucy chuckled. 'I'll try and remember that.'

Sally stood up. 'I'd better go and get changed. You did well, Lucy.' Impulsively she leaned forward and hugged the young mother, and Lucy hugged her back.

'Thank you just doesn't cover it.'

'I loved it,' Sally said simply, and Tom looked at her closely, seeing the brightness of her eyes.

Had it hurt her, seeing the baby born?

He knew how badly she'd always wanted children of her own. Part of him was surprised that she hadn't met someone on her travels and settled down.

And part of him was relieved.

He followed her out of the room just as she was tucking a tissue into her pocket.

His insides twisted and he resisted the temptation to haul her against him. The way things were between them at the moment, she'd slap his face.

'Sal?' His voice was soft. 'Is something wrong?'

Her slim shoulders tensed and then she turned and gave him a cool smile.

'Nothing at all. I'm going back to the unit now. I'll see you later.'

'Wait.' Tom caught her arm. 'Emma said that you can start your weekend early. They're quiet up there for once and you're off duty in a few hours anyway. She said that you were to go home. She'll see you on Monday.'

She digested this and then stirred slightly. 'Right.' She stepped neatly away from him, removing her arm from his grasp. 'I'll see you Monday, then.'

'How are you getting home?'

She looked at him blankly, as if the question hadn't occurred to her until that moment. 'I've got my bike.'

'I'll give you a lift,' he said immediately, and he braced himself for rejection as he saw her tense. 'You must be tired. We can drop some of the equipment off at the mountain rescue base on the way past.'

'I don't think so.' She turned and walked away from him, and he gritted his teeth with frustration.

She seemed determined not to spend one single second in his company, and her casual dismissal bruised his ego more than he cared to admit.

Seven years ago she'd adored him and hadn't been afraid to show it.

Now all she felt was indifference.

Or was it? His eyes narrowed as he contemplated an alternative explanation.

If she were truly indifferent to him, surely she'd be perfectly happy to accept a lift.

But if she wasn't indifferent…

If she was finding it as hard to be near to him as he was finding it to be near to her…

He watched her walk down the corridor, noticing the

swing of her hips and the way her blonde hair swung round her shoulders.

She was beautiful and she affected him as no other woman ever had. And there was one thing he now knew for sure.

If he'd ever thought he'd got over Sally, he'd been fooling himself.

CHAPTER FIVE

SALLY concentrated her attention on the rock, keeping her weight carefully balanced over her feet, as she looked for the next handhold.

One false move...

Just one false move and she'd plummet to the bottom because she'd chosen not to use the support of a rope.

It was just her and the rock-face.

A few more reaches and pulls and finally she was on top.

She closed her eyes and breathed in deeply, feeling the tension ooze out of her.

It was true that there was a lack of challenging climbing in the Lake District, but despite that she loved it here and at the moment she wouldn't swap it for the Himalayas or the Karakorum.

It felt like home.

'You shouldn't free climb. It's dangerous.' The deep, masculine voice came from directly behind her and she froze, recognizing Tom's voice without even turning to identify the speaker.

'What are you doing here?'

But it was a silly question.

This had been their place. Somewhere that both of them had loved. It was hardly surprising that he still came here.

'I was looking for you.' His tone was easy. 'I thought I'd find you here and I was right.'

Sally gritted her teeth, wishing that she'd been less predictable.

He sat down next to her, his dark hair windblown, his jaw dark with stubble. 'Do you remember how often we used to come here? It was our special place.'

The peace and comfort vanished in an instant and she scrambled to her feet, raking her blonde hair out of her eyes with a shaking hand.

'Don't get all sentimental on me, Tom,' she said coolly. 'I came here because it's a fun climb. Not because I want to wallow in the past. I don't.'

He nodded, his eyes steady on her face. 'And you needed to relax. It's been a tough week, Sally. Tough on both of us.'

She deliberately chose to misunderstand him. 'Yesterday was certainly a challenge.' She kept her tone neutral. 'But it had a happy ending. The baby is beautiful and they're doing fine—I called this morning to check.'

'You were amazing.' His voice was soft. 'Do you realize how much you've changed?'

She wished he wouldn't look at her like that, his sexy blue eyes fixed on her face as if he was seeking access to her every thought.

'Of course I've changed.' She released her blonde hair from its ponytail and shook it so that it trailed down her back and lifted in the wind. 'We've all changed, Tom. It's been seven years, and seven years is a long time.'

But not that long.

'Seven years ago you never would have been able to do what you did yesterday.'

'Of course not. I wasn't an experienced midwife.'

He shook his head. 'That's not what I mean. You've developed confidence, Sally. A belief in yourself. Something you didn't have seven years ago. Seven years ago you would have doubted your ability to deliver that baby in those circumstances. You would have been panicking.'

'Instead of which, you were the one doing the panicking.' She couldn't resist teasing him slightly. 'I've never seen you rattled before, Tom.'

'That was the most nerve-racking moment of my career,' he confessed in a rueful tone, and she looked at him, surprised to hear him admit it.

'Well, now who's changed?!' She lifted an eyebrow in challenge. 'You used to think that there was nothing you couldn't deal with.'

He gave a wry smile. 'There's arrogance for you.'

She frowned slightly at his response, still unable to understand why he'd been so tense. 'You deal with obstetric emergencies almost every day of your life.'

'That's right,' he drawled, 'in a modern, well-equipped hospital with every possible piece of machinery at my disposal, including an operating theatre. Just for the record, you probably ought to know that delivering a woman in precipitate labour on a mountain at the end of winter is not my idea of relaxation.'

Sally gave a wistful smile. 'Actually, I think it was wonderful.'

'Clearly. As I said, you were amazing.' He looked at her for a moment. 'Didn't you once think about all the possible things that could go wrong?'

She gave a faint smile. 'Of course. And then I dismissed those thoughts. I'm a midwife. I'm trained to believe that childbirth is a natural experience. You're an obstetrician. You're trained to believe that you're there to sort out problems. If there had been problems, I would have stood aside and handed over to you.'

Tom lifted an eyebrow. 'You think I can perform a Caesarean with a bar of chocolate and a penknife?'

She breathed in. 'I think you would have done whatever was necessary,' she said simply. 'I've never questioned your skills as a doctor, Tom.'

'Your faith in me is touching, especially given the fact that I left you to do all the work.' His firm mouth curved into a self-deprecating smile and she felt her heart kick against her chest.

She'd always loved his smile.

He looked wonderfully familiar in his mountain gear and she felt her memories collide inside her.

It seemed like yesterday that they'd sat here and planned the future.

Or rather, she'd planned the future.

A twinge of disquiet shot through her. She'd always talked about babies and family and it was only now that it occurred to her that Tom had said very little.

'You never wanted it, did you?' Her tone was hoarse as she voiced her thoughts. 'All those things we talked about. You never wanted the family. For you it was all about the job. Your career. Becoming the best.'

Tom was silent for a long moment, his eyes fixed on her face. 'That was part of it,' he admitted gruffly, 'but I wanted a family, too. One day. With a woman who loved me.'

She flinched as though he'd struck her. 'Are you saying that I didn't love you?'

'I know you thought you did. But you were young.' Tom turned to stare across the mountains, a muscle working in his rough jaw. 'I was the first man who'd made love to you, Sally. And you were just eighteen.'

She tried to keep her breathing steady but the memories were too powerful. 'You're trying to tell me that I didn't know my own mind?'

'You were desperate for love and a family. And I understood that. You were moved from one foster-home to another. It's hardly surprising that you dreamed of home and hearth. We were crazy about each other, but instead of enjoying the relationship you talked about nothing but babies and living together. I was the only man you'd ever been with. I was never sure if you wanted me for myself or because you saw me as a way to fulfil the dream you'd always had.'

She stood still with shock, frozen to the spot by his interpretation of what they'd shared, the delicate atmosphere between them shattered by his honesty.

He sucked in a breath. 'You were afraid, Sally. You didn't think you could exist on your own. You had no confidence or self-belief. Our relationship never would have worked under those circumstances. I was working hideous hours at the hospital and my mind was never on the job. I was always worrying about you. And all you could talk about was babies.'

She swallowed. 'I didn't ask you to worry about me.'

'Well, I did.' He rose to his feet and looked at her, his gaze direct. 'You wanted a family to replace what you'd never had, and I was supposed to provide that.'

'That's rubbish.' Her voice was hoarse and her heart was thumping as she backed away from him. 'I loved you. You're just trying to make yourself feel better about the fact that you ended it.'

He shook his head, his mouth set in a grim line. 'Believe me, nothing could make me feel better about ending our relationship. It was the hardest thing I ever did. But I know it was the right thing. Especially now, when I see the person you've grown into.'

Pain shafted through her but she lifted her chin and stared him in the eyes. 'That is so patronizing! So am I supposed to thank you?' Her voice shook with anger. 'Am I supposed to be grateful that you so generously threw away what I felt for you? You are so arrogant, Tom Hunter! You're just justifying the fact that your career mattered more than I did.'

She stalked away from him but he grabbed her arm, preventing her escape.

'That isn't true.' His voice was rough. 'You want the truth? Well, the truth was I was always afraid that one day you'd wake up and realize that there was a whole world out there. A world that you hadn't seen. I didn't want you to be with me just because I was the first and only man you'd ever been with. I didn't want you to be trapped with a young family when you were so young yourself. I wanted you to see life first.'

Her heart was thumping so hard that she felt strange. 'I was with you because I loved you. You were my life, Tom. My whole world. I wasn't interested in the rest of it.'

She shook his arm away and stepped backwards.

How could he even *begin* to justify the decision he'd made?

She still couldn't understand how he could have wrecked something that had seemed so perfect.

'I didn't expect you to leave,' he said hoarsely. 'I didn't want that. All I wanted was breathing space—I wanted to be sure that it was the right thing. For both of us.'

'You didn't expect me to leave?' She set her chin at a dangerous angle and her eyes flashed. 'You thought I'd sit around and watch while you dated other women?'

He sucked in a breath. 'I didn't date anyone, Sally. Not in the way that you mean.'

She didn't even want to think about it.

Spitting fire and flame, she turned on her heel but he grabbed her again.

'Don't walk away from this.'

'I'm walking away for your sake because if I don't walk away I'm going to injure you!' Her eyes flashed into his and she struggled to steady her breathing. 'I actually do now feel like blacking your eye, but I don't want to be on the receiving end of the speculation that your black eye would undoubtedly receive in this small community.'

'Well, before you walk just think about this…' His voice was weary and his fingers bit into her arm. 'Think about all the things you've done in the last seven years and then ask yourself if you'd have done any of them if we'd stayed together.'

She stared at him for a long moment, her breathing rapid, and then she tugged her arm away from him and stalked down the path, the set of her shoulders warning him not to follow her.

How dared he say those things?

He was implying that he'd done her a favour by ending their relationship.

Sally walked quickly, trying to escape from the thoughts that crowded her brain, but they rolled around inside her head, crying out for attention.

She reached her bike and swung her leg over the saddle, pausing for a moment as Tom's words came back to her with brutal clarity.

I was never sure if you wanted me for myself or because you saw me as a way to fulfil the dream you'd always had.

Her hands tightened on the handlebars and she sucked in a breath.

Even as part of her insisted that he'd just been trying to justify his actions, another part of her questioned whether there might not have been some truth in what he'd said.

Had she just been desperate to create the family that she'd never had?

It was certainly true that Tom had been the first person in her life that she'd loved.

And it was true that all she'd ever wanted had been a family. She'd spent her entire childhood on the fringes of other people's families and she'd dreamed about being in the centre of her own. Of mattering to someone.

And she'd mattered to Tom.

For the first time in her life, someone had taken an interest in her and loved her.

Had that love stifled him? Put pressure on him?

Disturbed by the thoughts running through her mind, Sally stirred and fastened her cycle helmet, determined not to spend any more time dwelling on the past.

It was the future that mattered, and the future meant finding somewhere to live. She still had the rest of the day in which to find a flat, and she intended to do just that.

Whatever had happened between her and Tom was in the past, and that was where it was staying.

Tom ran a hand over his face and cursed softly.

He could go after her, of course, but he knew that there was no point in trying to continue the conversation until she'd had time to calm down and think about the things he'd said.

So he watched in silence as her slender, super-fit figure disappeared into the distance, remembering the pleasure he'd derived from watching her climb after so many years.

Some climbers seemed to heave themselves upwards in a series of dramatic jerks, but when Sally climbed it was like watching a mixture of ballet and gymnastics. Her movements were smooth and measured, her body strong and athletic as she pitted herself against the rock-face.

She might not want to accept that she'd changed, but she had.

Tom gave a wry smile as he accepted the inevitable consequence of that change. She no longer needed him.

The days when she'd asked his opinion on anything and everything were obviously long gone.

This new Sally seemed to know exactly what she wanted.

And at the moment it wasn't him.

He stared at the mountains, breathing in the air, enjoying the solitude. So much of his relationship with Sally had been forged in these mountains. They'd shared so much, understood each other's need to climb and be outdoors.

His eyes drifted down the sharp line of a ridge straight ahead and he wondered if that was one of the reasons why he'd never managed to make a commitment to another woman.

For a while Sally had been part of him. She'd understood who he was. Everything about him. And he hadn't come close to sharing that bond with any other woman.

And he didn't want to.

The realization hit him like a physical blow.

He still wanted Sally.

And ending their relationship seven years ago had

been the biggest mistake of his life. He should have married her while he'd had the chance and given her so many babies that she couldn't leave the house!

He ran a hand over his face and cursed softly.

Maybe she was right. Maybe he had been arrogant, making the decision for both of them. Maybe he should have trusted her feelings more.

Trusted her love for him.

But he hadn't, and he'd thrown away the one thing that had mattered to him in life.

He sucked in a deep breath and stared across the mountains without seeing their beauty.

For seven years he'd had to live with the lingering doubt that he'd made the wrong decision and there hadn't been anything he'd been able to do about it.

But she'd finally come back.

Sally Jenner was home.

Which meant that he'd been given a second chance.

By the time she returned to work on the following Monday, Sally was feeling more positive.

She'd found a lovely garden flat on the shores of the lake, which was available immediately, and she intended to move in as soon as possible.

She'd taken Bryony and Helen to see it and both of them had agreed that it was idyllic. And Sally was already forming a close friendship with Helen. She could see what Oliver loved about her. She was gentle and warm and extremely good company.

And as the three of them had stood staring at the view from Sally's new flat, Helen had asked her if she'd be one of her bridesmaids. Bryony and her seven-year-old daughter, Lizzie, had already agreed.

'I don't have sisters,' Helen said quietly, 'and I've

always wanted three bridesmaids. Don't ask me why. Will you do it?'

Sally had hesitated but Helen had been so sweetly insistent that eventually she'd agreed.

'Sally?' Emma walked up to her, carrying a pile of notes, a harassed expression on her face. 'A woman's just turned up complaining of breathlessness and chest pains. The husband says that they've given up on the GP because he just keeps giving them different antibiotics. He's obviously really worried about her. Would you check her blood pressure and things while I just call Tom?'

'Of course. Is she booked with us?'

'No.' Emma shook her head. 'They're staying with family but I think she is carrying her notes. The husband told me that she's thirty-three weeks. First baby.'

Sally hurried to the examination room and introduced herself to the couple. 'How long have you been this breathless, Mrs Singh?'

'For about a month.' The woman was overcome by a severe bout of coughing and Sally frowned.

'And you've seen your doctor?'

The husband nodded. 'He said that she has a chest infection and he's given her two different types of antibiotics. She was feeling a little better yesterday so we came up to stay with my brother, but suddenly in the night she was much worse.'

'And you've had pains in your chest?' Sally checked the woman's temperature, pulse and blood pressure and offered her a drink as she started to cough again. 'Mrs Singh, can you describe the pain in your chest?'

The woman gave an agonized gasp. 'It happens when I breathe in. Such a sharp pain. The GP said it was infection.'

Sally nodded and quickly scanned the notes. 'And when you cough, are you bringing anything up?'

Her husband nodded. 'All night she coughed up clear, frothy stuff.'

Sally tucked some pillows behind the woman and gave her a smile. 'Try not to worry. I'm going to find the consultant now and ask him to come and take a look at you. Then we'll get you sorted out.'

She hurried onto the labour ward in search of Tom and saw him emerge from Theatre, a mask dangling round his neck.

'Are you looking for me?'

He looked tough, male and far too tempting for her peace of mind.

Her heart kicked against her chest but she ignored the reaction and concentrated on the problem in hand.

'There's a woman in the examination room complaining of chest pain and difficulty breathing,' she told him quickly. 'Her GP has treated her with two lots of antibiotics.'

Tom lifted an eyebrow. 'But?'

'I don't think she has a chest infection,' Sally said immediately. 'I think her symptoms might be cardiac.'

The moment she'd said the words she wished she hadn't. She wasn't a doctor and the woman's GP had diagnosed a chest infection. What reason did she have to doubt him?

She waited stiffly for Tom to dismiss her assessment of the patient but he didn't. Instead, his gaze fixed on hers intently.

'Why do you think it's cardiac?'

'Because she's coughing up clear, frothy sputum, she has tachycardia and she's describing pleuritic chest pain,' Sally said immediately. 'I think she's showing signs of pulmonary oedema. I've seen it before. I'm wondering whether she has rheumatic heart disease.'

'You've seen it before?' Tom frowned. 'Mitral stenosis in British women is pretty rare.'

'She was born in Pakistan and I saw several similar cases when I was working in a clinic there. It seems to be more common in Asian women. I have a bad feeling about her.'

Tom didn't hesitate. 'So let's go and see her together and if necessary we'll get the cardiologists involved. Did anyone listen to her heart when she booked?'

'Yes, but there's nothing in the notes.'

'I'll just grab a stethoscope and I'll meet you in the room.'

Mrs Singh was coughing again when Tom walked into the room and Sally felt her heart skip a beat.

What if she was wrong?

What if it was just a simple chest infection that hadn't cleared with the antibiotics?

Perhaps she was being over-dramatic.

Tom questioned the couple carefully and then listened to the woman's chest, his face expressionless as he concentrated on the sounds.

Finally he straightened. 'I want to run a few more tests, Mrs Singh,' he said calmly. 'I want you to have a chest X-ray and an echocardiogram, and I'm going to ask the cardiologist to come and see you straight away. I think the problem may be your heart rather than your lungs. I just need to talk to my colleague while Sally arranges for your X-ray, and then we'll talk again.'

Sally followed him out of the room and across to the desk.

'It's OK for her to have an X-ray?' Sally put the form under his nose and he scribbled on it quickly.

'She's in her third trimester so it's fine. And it's essential that we see what's going on.'

'But you do think it is her heart?'

'If you're asking whether I think you're clever, the answer is yes, Sally Jenner.' He dropped the pen back on the desk and gave a crooked smile. 'Very clever. Cleverer than the GP who has been treating her for a chest infection.'

'Well, I've probably seen more cases than he has,' Sally said practically, opening the phone book and sticking it under his nose. 'As you say, it isn't such a common problem in this country. I suppose you want to call the cardiologist. I'm afraid I don't know who he is. I haven't been here long enough to find out.'

'It's a she,' Tom said immediately, something flickering in his blue eyes, 'and her name is Chantal Mornington. She's half-French.'

And Tom liked her. That much was obvious.

Not liking the feeling of jealousy that stabbed through her, Sally forced a smile. 'Are you going to call her or shall I?'

'I'll call her and talk to her about the echo—you sort out the chest X-ray. I want to see that before I speak to Chantal.'

Wondering just what Chantal Mornington was to Tom, Sally made the necessary arrangements and stayed with Mrs Singh while she went to X-ray.

Tom was waiting for the films when she arrived back on the unit. She handed them over and he examined them in silence, his expression intent.

'Well?' Sally glanced at him expectantly and he stirred.

'She has an enlarged left atrium and some shadowing here...' He tapped with his pen, and then glanced over his shoulder with a smile as an elegant, dark-haired woman walked up to the desk. 'Chantal. Thanks for coming.'

'As if I'd refuse. You're one of the few of my colleagues who doesn't waste my time.' Her voice was smoky and seductive and Sally felt as though she'd stepped naked into a mountain stream.

There was no mistaking the beautiful cardiologist's feelings for Tom and, judging from the warmth in his eyes, he wasn't exactly immune either.

'We seem to have a case of pulmonary oedema due to mitral stenosis,' he said, and Chantal stepped closer, her body brushing against his as she took a closer look at the X-ray.

'I've seen one or two similar cases in my career,' she said smoothly, 'but it's actually quite rare in this country now. You did well to spot it, Tom.'

Her dark eyes glowed with approval and invitation and Tom smiled down at her before turning briefly to Sally.

'Actually, Sally was the one who picked it up,' he said easily. 'She's worked in Pakistan and she's seen it before in young Asian women. Very smart of her.'

'Indeed.' The cardiologist's eyes slid to Sally and then away again, dismissing her as unimportant.

'You'll want to do an echo, of course,' Tom said, 'and I suppose we ought to start her on beta-blockers.'

They spoke about the management for a few minutes, their heads close together, and Sally decided it was time to remind them that she existed.

'Why beta-blockers?'

Tom dragged his gaze away from the beautiful cardiologist. 'Because as her heart rate increases so her stroke volume falls, and that puts increasing pressure on the left atrium,' he explained. 'All of those effects can be reversed by the use of beta-blockers.'

'That's why I like working with you,' Chantal said huskily, removing the X-ray from the light box and slipping it into its cover. 'Very few obstetricians understand even the most basic principles of cardiology. We'll move her to CCU, do the echo and see if she's suitable for a balloon valvuloplasty. Are you happy with her from an obstetric point of view?'

'For the time being.' Tom nodded. 'We'll want to monitor the baby, obviously.'

'You know you're always welcome on my unit,' Chantal murmured silkily. 'Are you going to argue with me if I start her on diuretics?'

'I'd be uneasy.' Tom frowned. 'Hypovolaemia will reduce the placental blood flow and that could have a detrimental effect on the foetus.'

Chantal smiled. 'In that case, I'll assess the degree of pulmonary congestion and talk to you before I do anything. Agreed?'

'Agreed.' He smiled. 'Thanks, Chantal.'

Resisting the temptation to grind her teeth, Sally excused herself and went back to tell Mrs Singh what was happening, trying hard not to analyse her feelings.

Why should she care if Chantal Mornington clearly had a serious crush on Tom?

And why should she care if those feelings were reciprocated?

The guy was bound to have a love life of some sort, and they were welcome to each other.

She really didn't care.

So why did she suddenly feel so crushed?

Trying hard to pull herself together, she helped transfer Mrs Singh to CCU and then returned to the labour ward.

'Grab a cup of coffee while it's quiet,' Emma suggested, and Sally gave a nod and made her way to the staffroom.

She stopped dead when she saw Tom sprawled in one of the armchairs. He was scanning a medical journal and nursing a cup of coffee. He glanced up and saw her and his blue gaze was suddenly warm.

'Hello, there.' He uncoiled his length and stood up, dropping the journal on the coffee-table. 'Can I pour you a coffee?'

She was tempted to refuse but she didn't want him questioning her reaction so she nodded instead, forcing herself to walk into the room. 'Black, please. No sugar.'

He reached for a mug and filled it. 'So you came across pulmonary oedema in Pakistan?'

She took the mug. 'Thanks, and to answer your question, yes, I did. The medical workers seemed to think that mitral valve disease was on the increase. We had a few women who came in with problems in their pregnancy.'

Tom nodded. 'The rise in cardiac output puts a tremendous stress on the heart. Patients can often deteriorate suddenly and unexpectedly, and if a diagnosis isn't made quickly enough, the consequences are serious.'

Sally sipped her coffee. 'I certainly saw a couple of cases similar to Mrs Singh's. Do you think she'll be OK?'

'Who knows?' He shrugged his broad shoulders. 'But Chantal Mornington is an excellent cardiologist.'

'Yes. I could see that you had quite a mutual appreciation society going on,' Sally said tartly, and then wished she hadn't spoken as he turned amused blue eyes in her direction.

'Meaning?'

She shrugged, cursing herself for making such an impulsive remark. 'Nothing.'

He was silent for a moment and then he put his coffee-mug down on the table and leaned towards her, his gaze searching.

'If you're suggesting what I think you're suggesting, I could say that you're being ridiculous—' his voice was soft '—or I could say that I'm pleased that you are jealous.'

She stiffened. 'I'm not jealous.'

'No?'

'No. There's nothing between us any more, Tom. You're perfectly entitled to see anyone you like.'

And she was going to do the same.

Any day now she was going to meet someone.

'That's a lie.'

'You think you need my permission to date?'

He was silent for a moment and when he spoke his voice had lost all traces of humour. 'There's only one woman I intend to date and I'm looking at her.'

For a few, frantic beats her heart suddenly lost its natural rhythm. 'You can't be serious.'

'I'm perfectly serious. And if you're about to pretend that there's nothing between us, I ought to warn you that you're wasting your time. It's been there from the moment we met and it will always be there.'

She stood up so abruptly that the chair scraped on the floor. 'Just in case you need reminding, we've been here before, Tom, and it didn't work. And now I need to get back to work.'

'I know I hurt you badly,' he said softly, 'but it was a long time ago and we've both changed, Sally.'

'That's right,' she said hoarsely. 'Fortunately we have both changed. I'm no longer stupid enough to fall in love with a man who doesn't want that love. I'm not making that mistake again.'

He flinched and rose to his feet, walking round the table towards her. 'The only mistake was mine. But at the time I thought I was making the right decision. You were so young, Sally—'

'No!' She raised a hand to keep him at a distance. 'I don't want to hear your excuses when the truth is that I just didn't fit into your agenda at the time.'

He looked at her, a tiny muscle flickering in his jaw. 'So you're truly pretending that there's nothing between us?'

'I don't need to pretend. I know.'

He took a step closer to her, his voice low and husky. 'You don't feel anything when I walk into a room?'

Her heart was thumping so hard she was surprised he couldn't see it. 'Nothing at all.'

'Right.'

She had a brief glimpse of burning blue eyes and a devil's smile and then his hand slid round the back of her neck and his mouth came down on hers.

Her soft gasp of shock turned to a moan as he took what he wanted. His kiss was all fire and heat and he held her head still with one strong hand as his mouth stole and plundered. With the erotic probe of his tongue he robbed her of breath and willpower, and with the brush of his lips he took her power of speech.

White heat exploded through her body and she placed a hand on his chest, feeling the hardness of muscle and the throb of his heart. Her body was screaming for more and she gave a tiny sob of protest as he dragged his mouth from hers, his breathing unsteady.

For a long, sexually charged moment neither of them spoke.

Neither of them was able to speak.

And then his hand dropped from her head, thick dark lashes shielding the expression in his blue eyes as he looked down at her. 'Seven years ago I made a mistake, Sally. But I'm not making that same mistake a second time. I'm coming after you.' His voice was very male and very sexy. 'And no matter how fast you run, I'm going to catch you. And once I've caught you, I'm never letting you go.'

CHAPTER SIX

The call out came in the middle of the night but Sally hadn't slept.

She'd lain awake, staring into the darkness, thinking of that kiss.

It wasn't fair.

Nature had it all wrong. It shouldn't be possible to respond to someone who had caused such emotional trauma.

The body should have some inbuilt self-preservation mechanism that prevented it from feeling passion for the wrong person.

And Tom Hunter was definitely the wrong person.

She lifted the receiver on the second ring, her voice gruff with tiredness. 'Hello?'

It was Sean, the mountain rescue team leader, telling her about a call out.

Sally sat up in bed and stifled a yawn. 'I'll meet you at the base as soon as I can. I'll have to cycle.'

Sean's voice was clear and crisp down the phone. 'Tom will pick you up. He's already on his way.'

Remembering his promise that he was coming after her, Sally's heart skipped a beat.

He obviously hadn't lost any time in looking for opportunities for being alone with her.

She ended her conversation with Sean, dressed quickly and made herself a piece of toast while she waited for the sound of Tom's car.

Then she told herself firmly that the pleasure of the

kiss wasn't worth the pain of a relationship. There was no way she'd put herself in that position again.

He'd ended it once before, he could end it again.

By the time he arrived she had herself firmly in hand. She reached for her coat, locked the door to the cottage and met him before he'd even stopped the car.

'Thanks for the lift. It saved me some time.' She gave him a cool smile and then gasped as he reached for her and pulled her against him.

His mouth found hers in a kiss that was as brief as it was devastating.

Her head spun and heat flared low in her pelvis.

'Something on account for later,' he said roughly, releasing her before she had the satisfaction of pulling away.

She sat in frozen silence, dealing with the sudden race of her heart and the spread of warmth through her body.

He glanced at her, amusement in his blue eyes. 'You'd better put your seat belt on. The roads might be icy.'

Hating herself for responding to him and hating him even more for noticing, she did as he'd instructed, her hands shaking slightly as she fastened the seat belt.

She was going to ignore it.

She was going to pretend that both kisses had never happened.

'Do we know what this call out is all about?' She tugged her blonde hair into a ponytail and then wedged it neatly under a fleece hat.

'Two kids were seen walking up on the ridge just before sunset. They haven't returned and there have been several reports of flashing lights.'

'Right.' Sally was twisting this way and that, pulling on different pieces of clothing and generally getting herself ready for freezing weather. 'Are we using a dog team?'

He nodded. 'Ellie is bringing Max.'

Sally frowned. 'Isn't it a bit soon? Bryony tells me that Ellie only had her baby a couple of months ago.'

'The baby is fine. Ben is staying with him.'

Sally glanced at him. 'I gather you were a bit of a hero. You sectioned Ellie.'

His hands tightened on the wheel. 'She had a car accident in the last month of her pregnancy. Her placenta came away—it was an emergency. Stop changing the subject. I'm not going to let you ignore it, Sally.'

Her heart skipped a beat at his swift change of subject. 'Ignore what?'

'The fact that the temperature rises when we're within touching distance, the fact that when I kiss you, you still want me as much as I want you.' He glanced across at her, his blue gaze glittering in the semi-darkness. 'Whether you like it or not, that kiss proved something.'

'It proved that you still know how to kiss a woman.' She kept her tone light. 'That's all it proved. Glad to know you haven't lost your touch, Tom.'

He swore under his breath and turned into the car park of the mountain rescue base. 'We can't talk about this now.'

'I don't want to talk about it at all,' she muttered, undoing her seat belt and opening the car door before he'd even put the handbrake on. 'And if you're coming after me, Tom Hunter, you'd better be fit.'

She'd slammed the door and was across the car park before he had time to answer.

'We know who they are now,' Sean told everyone as they gathered in the briefing room. 'James Knight and his friend Lester Roberts. James's mother called us five minutes ago and said that they'd been missing since tea-time. Apparently there was a huge family row—she wouldn't say what about and she didn't contact the police before now because she thought James would come home.'

'So how do we know they're the same kids who were seen on the ridge?' Tom zipped up his jacket and reached for his rucksack.

'Because, when James didn't come home, his mother searched his room and found all his walking gear missing. Then she called Lester's mother and discovered that he was gone, too. They're assuming that they've gone into the hills.'

'And she didn't say what the row was about?' Sally looked at Sean and he shook his head.

'She's obviously hideously embarrassed about all the fuss. And I don't suppose any family likes washing their dirty laundry in public. She didn't want to go into detail and I didn't see the point of asking. A row is a row. The kid's gone. We need to find him. And the friend he dragged along with him.'

'But it might be important,' Sally began, and Sean nodded.

'I'm sure it is. But what matters for now is finding them before they freeze to death out there or lose their footing. We've had reports of lights in two different places so we're going to split up. If they're up on the ridge in this weather, they'll be in trouble.'

He gave the whole team their instructions and they set off, lights shining from their helmets as they walked.

Ellie immediately slid in beside Sally and Tom, a happy smile on her face. 'Can't believe you're back,

Sal.' She gave her a quick hug and then turned to Tom and put a hand on her chest. 'And hello to my hero.'

Tom gave a wry smile. 'Don't start, Ellie.'

Undaunted, Ellie looked at Sally. 'Has he told you that he saved my life?'

'I heard it from other sources. He didn't tell me himself.'

Ellie's gaze softened. 'He's too modest.'

'Really?' Sally's tone was tart and she looked at Tom with challenge in her green eyes. 'From where I'm standing, he seems to think he's God's gift.'

Ellie laughed. 'Like that, is it?' She stooped to give her dog a quick pat as they moved quickly up the path. 'Well, he saved my life, and Ethan's life, so you won't be hearing me doing anything but sing his praises. I was driving along, minding my own business, and this tree leapt out in front of me.'

'Women drivers,' Tom drawled, but there was a genuine affection in his eyes as he looked at Ellie.

'You can't provoke me, Tom Hunter. You saved my life so now you own me.' Ellie frowned thoughtfully. 'Or do I own you? I can't remember how that proverb goes, but I think one of us owns the other.'

Sally laughed. 'I think Ben might object to either version.'

'I don't want to own you, Ellie,' Tom said dryly, 'you talk too much. I'd strangle you after five minutes. Even when we were trying to gas you before your section, your mouth was still moving.'

'I was nervous,' Ellie admitted happily, 'but you made me feel better about the whole thing. You were very macho and in charge, Tom. You do the whole "lean on me" thing really well. If I'd met you before Ben, I would have had a serious crush on you.'

Sally choked back a laugh. She loved the fact that Ellie was so frank and honest about everything.

'Ellie.' Tom's voice was weary. 'Just shut up, will you? There's a drop here, and if you don't concentrate you'll go over the edge.'

'I can walk and talk,' Ellie said firmly, and Sally smiled.

For all her lovable chatter, Ellie obviously hero-worshipped Tom.

And once so had she.

When she'd been eighteen she'd thought he was some sort of god.

She frowned slightly, walking steadily in the darkness, following Ellie and Tom. She couldn't stop thinking of the things he'd said to her on top of their rock. Had she put too much pressure on him? He'd always been so confident and in control, it had never occurred to her that he might have doubts of any sort.

Had she been unrealistic about their relationship?

She walked in silence for a while, aware of Ellie chattering away in the background.

And then suddenly a brief flash of light caught her eye.

She stopped dead, her eyes fixed on a spot ahead of them. 'I saw something.'

Tom turned to her. 'Where?'

'Higher up.'

He frowned. 'The path is very narrow there.'

'I saw something,' Sally said firmly, her eyes searching the darkness for another flash of light.

Ellie spoke to Max and the dog shot off. He was wearing a high-visibility coat with bells attached and a green chemical light that glowed in the darkness.

'He looks like an alien,' Tom muttered, but Ellie's attention was fixed on the dog.

He moved further away from them and for a moment all they could see was the green glow of the light.

Then he bounded back and barked at Ellie.

'He's found them,' she said immediately, bending to praise the dog. 'Better let the others know.'

The wind gusted violently and Sally staggered slightly. Instantly Tom's hand shot out and he steadied her.

'We should rope up here,' he said gruffly, swinging the rucksack off his back and delving for the necessary equipment. 'The path narrows here and it's badly eroded. I'm not taking any chances in the dark.'

They sorted out their own safety and then Ellie led the way, following Max until they reached a figure huddled down on the path.

'One of them. Only one of them.' Sally dropped to her knees beside the boy. 'Are you Lester or James?'

He was shivering too badly to speak to her and Tom immediately handed her some extra layers which she wrapped carefully round the child.

'You're going to be fine,' she said soothingly, 'and we're going to get you down. Where's your friend?'

The boy turned his eyes to hers and in the light from her helmet she could see that he was white and shaking. His eyes turned to the path. 'He went over the edge...'

Sally felt a chill run through her that was nothing to do with the icy wind. 'Over the edge? All right—well, we'll sort him out, too. But are you Lester or James?'

'I'm James.' The words were little more than a whisper and they were all but swallowed by the howl of the wind. 'And this is my fault. It's all my fault. He came with me. And he fell.'

The boy was clearly shocked and on the edges of hypothermia himself. Sally slipped an arm around him. 'Don't worry, James. We're going to find your friend. In the meantime, we need to get you down to safer ground. It's a bit risky up here with this wind.'

She straightened and let Ellie take over while she, Sean and Tom moved to one side to plan.

'If he's gone over the edge here, he's gone all the way to the bottom,' Sean said grimly, and Sally shook her head.

'Not necessarily. There's a rocky outcrop halfway down. I know because I ate a sandwich there once.'

Tom raised an eyebrow. 'Only you would picnic on a sheer face.'

'There was a good view.' Sally was still staring into the darkness, hoping to see something. 'On the other hand, he might have gone straight to the bottom.'

Sean shouted over the edge and flashed his torch, but there was no response.

'I've got a more powerful torch.' Tom reached into his rucksack and retrieved another torch, which he shone down the side of the cliff. Immediately there was an answering flash. 'You're right. He's there.'

Ellie had joined them.

'We'll need to go down to him,' she said immediately, but Tom shook his head.

'As your surgeon, I'm telling you that you're not going anywhere. I don't mind you walking a couple of months after your Caesarean but I draw the line at lowering you down a cliff on the end of a rope.'

Ellie grinned cheekily. 'Are you doubting your sewing skills?'

'Call me fussy but I just don't fancy restitching your uterus halfway up a cliff face,' Tom said dryly. 'I'll go.'

Sean nodded. 'Sounds good to me. Get roped up. Ellie, you look after James. Get some fluids into him and if he's up to it, you and Toby rope him up and bring him down lower.'

They swung into action, operating with smooth efficiency, and within minutes Tom was stepping boldly over the edge of the sheer drop.

Sally felt her heart lurch and Ellie put a hand on her arm.

'He'll be fine.'

Sally lifted her chin and shrugged slightly. 'I'm not worried about him.'

'You're a hopeless liar, Sally Jenner,' Ellie said softly. 'You two are crazy about each other and always have been.'

'I'm not crazy about him,' Sally said hoarsely, watching as Sean skilfully masterminded the whole operation, getting people ready to act on Tom's instructions. 'And he ended our relationship, if you remember, so he's hardly crazy about me either.'

'Oh, men often get confused about what they really want,' Ellie said airily. 'It's up to us women to show them as tactfully as possible. And if tact doesn't work, just tell them straight out. It always amazes me how some men can be so clever and yet be so stupid when it comes to emotional stuff. Bless. It's amazing the human race continues.'

Sally laughed. 'You are priceless, Ellie MacAllister.'

'He's down.' Sean lifted a hand in their direction. He listened on the radio and beckoned to Sally. 'He needs another pair of hands and he says the ledge is narrow.'

'I'll go,' Sally said immediately, standing still while Sean checked the knots in her rope.

Then she went over the edge into the darkness, feeling a sudden gust of wind threaten to take her.

Tom shone the torch so that she could see what she was doing, and she abseiled quickly but carefully down the steep face, thankful that the visibility was good.

She could see Tom resting one foot on a narrow ledge, holding onto the shivering figure of the other boy.

'So this is Lester?'

'Presumably.' Tom raised his voice to be heard above the wind. 'I can't get him to speak or move. He just keeps shivering and clutching his side. I need to see if he's injured, but this rock isn't wide enough for me.'

'But it's wide enough for me,' Sally said immediately, shifting her position and stepping gingerly onto the rock next to the boy.

'Whatever you do, don't unclip your own rope,' Tom shouted grimly, and she looked at him.

'Do I look stupid?'

To her surprise he grinned. 'Actually, you look beautiful. A bit windblown maybe, but...' He shrugged and despite the seriousness of the situation she felt her heart warm.

Then she forced her attention back to the job in hand.

And the most important task was to get a rope onto Lester so that he was safe if something happened to his precarious perch.

'Lester, I'm Sally. I need to slip this over you so that we can get you safely attached to a rope.'

His teeth were chattering. 'I'm going to fall again.'

'You're not going to fall, sweetheart,' Sally said firmly, manoeuvring herself on the rock again so that she could slide the harness onto him. After several abortive attempts she managed it and clipped on the rope. Tom gave a nod of approval.

'Good job.' He spoke to Sean on the radio while Sally tried to work out how badly Lester had hurt himself.

'The rocks must have broken your fall,' she said. 'How did you land? Where does it hurt?'

The boy gave a gasp. 'My side.'

Sally nodded. 'Anywhere else?'

The boy shook his head and Tom moved closer so that he could take a look.

'There's no bleeding that I can see,' he said finally, 'but we need to get him off this ledge before things get worse.'

Sally gave a nod of understanding. The wind was rising, the temperature was dropping and nothing could be done for the boy in such an exposed and dangerous place.

'We can raise him or lower him,' she said, and Tom nodded, his hand still on the radio. 'Sean is sending down a stretcher.'

The radio crackled again and Tom spoke for a few seconds and then turned to Sally.

'They've got a problem up top. Can you go back up straight away?'

She frowned. 'Will you be all right here?'

His blue eyes mocked her. 'Worried about me, Sally Jenner?'

She bit her lip. 'No.'

'You're lying.' Even with the wind howling she could hear the change in his tone. 'And we're going to talk about it later.'

Sally cursed herself for revealing too much.

Knowing that she was going to pay for it later, she got on with the job.

Back on the ledge Ellie and Sean were huddled together, arguing about something.

'What's happening?' Sally unclipped her rope and walked over to them.

'James is refusing to go down, that's what's happening.' Sean ground his teeth in irritation and Ellie rolled her eyes.

'Men. Just leave it to us girls, Sean, darling.' She turned to Sally, her expression serious. 'Will you talk to him? He's really upset and muttering something about not belonging.' She reached out and put a hand on Sally's arm, her expression gentle. 'I know that's your specialist subject, Sally.'

Sally gave a rueful smile and a nod. 'It's nice to know that having a disastrous childhood can come in handy occasionally.'

'Just tell the kid that we need to get him off this mountain,' Sean said grimly, concentrating his attention on the stretcher that the other members of the team were lowering. 'By the time Tom gets his friend up here, I want him to move. Or I'll peel him off the ridge myself.'

Sally picked her way back along the exposed path to where the boy was still huddled, this time protected by several warm jackets.

'Hello, James. My friend Ellie tells me you don't want to go down.'

He gave a huge sniff. 'What's the point?'

'Well, because a lot of people love you and a lot of people are very worried about you,' she said gently, watching his face carefully. She couldn't remember how old Sean had said he was but, whatever his age, at the moment he just looked like a very young, very vulnerable child.

Her heart twisted with sympathy. Behind her she was aware of movement and activity as the rest of the team worked to lift the injured boy clear of the rock, but all her attention was fixed on James.

'Why would they want me?' His voice cracked and his eyes closed. As if he didn't want her to see what he was feeling. 'They told me today that I was adopted. They waited fourteen years to tell me and they told me today.'

Sally heard the agony in his voice and was silent for a moment. 'That's pretty tough.'

'Yeah.' James brushed his hand across his eyes and struggled for control. 'And it explains a lot. Why I always felt different. They wanted stuff from me that I couldn't do. My dad is a big footballer and he's always saying, ''Why can't you be more like me?'' and things like that. Well, it's not surprising I'm not like him, is it?'

He opened his eyes and looked at her, and Sally let out a breath, knowing that it would be so easy to say the wrong thing. To make it worse. 'I'm no expert on parents,' she said finally, 'because I never knew mine at all.'

He shivered inside the oversized jacket. 'You were adopted, too?'

She gave a wry smile, aware that Tom was now behind her. She ignored him, sensing that they weren't going to complete this rescue until James had been allowed to talk his problem through.

'I wasn't that lucky.' She couldn't keep the wistful note out of her voice. 'In fact, my whole childhood was spent dreaming that someone would *want* to adopt me. That someone would like me enough to want me to be part of their family.'

How could it still feel so raw after all these years?

Why didn't it ever go away?

She felt Tom's hand slide around her shoulder and hold her tightly, and for once she didn't feel like pushing him away.

James was staring at her. 'You really *wanted* to be adopted?'

'Oh, yes. I really did.' She gave a wan smile. 'People who adopt children really, *really* want them.'

James sat in silence, a frown on his face. 'But no one adopted you?'

She shook her head. 'No.' She kept her tone light. 'No one wanted me that badly.'

She thought she heard Tom swear softly behind her but she didn't turn. All her attention was still focused on James.

'So, if you weren't adopted, who looked after you? Where did you live?'

She gave a casual shrug that belied the pain of her childhood. 'With anyone who would have me. I was moved from foster-home to foster-home and spent some time in a children's home. It was pretty grim. But I had good friends.'

'Didn't you ever wonder about your real mum?'

She nodded. 'Of course. Who wouldn't? But adoption seemed so special to me. It meant that someone had chosen you.' She gave a wobbly smile. 'I mean, that's pretty amazing, don't you think? A couple decide that you're what they want, more than anything in the world.'

James was silent. 'But my real mother gave me away.'

Sally nodded. 'Maybe. Or maybe your real mother is the woman who fed you and changed you when you were a baby, who picked you up when you fell over and who now nags you to do your homework. Sounds to me as though she loves you very much.'

'She should have told me before.'

Sally gave a wan smile. 'Yes, she probably should. But I don't suppose there's ever a good time and nobody is perfect. Haven't you ever done something and then wished you'd done it differently?'

James thought and then nodded. 'I suppose so.'

'I know I have.' Aware that the temperature was falling, Sally reached for the boy's hand and gave it a squeeze. 'I know you're upset and you've certainly got plenty that you need to talk about with your mum and dad, but you can't do that up here.'

'They're going to be mad with me.'

'And that shows that they care,' Sally said quietly, still holding his hand. 'They're mad with you because they're worried, and they're worried because they love you. And I know you love them, too. And now we need to get you off this mountain. Lester's hurt himself, James. He's been a good friend to you and now you need to be a good friend to him. You need to come with me so that we can get you safely home and get Lester to the hospital.'

James stared at her. 'He isn't dead?'

'No, sweetheart,' Sally leaned forward and gave him a hug. 'He isn't dead. But we need to get him down.'

James closed his eyes and gave a choked sob. 'I thought I'd killed him. He came up here because I needed a friend.'

Sally nodded and released him. 'And what a great friend he is. I'd say you're a pretty lucky boy. People choose who they're friends with, and he chose you.'

James brushed the tears from his eyes and tried to stare along the path. 'So what happens now?'

'What happens now is that we're going to get you down,' Sally said firmly. 'And then, if you want to talk a bit more about feeling as though you don't belong, I'm your woman.'

CHAPTER SEVEN

'HE'S still in surgery,' Tom said, pacing the staffroom in the A and E department. 'Are you sure it was a ruptured spleen?'

'I'm an A and E consultant,' Jack said mildly. 'I think I can recognize the signs of a ruptured spleen. Presumably you can, too, which is why you cannulated the boy on the mountain and got him down here fast. I'm sure he'll be fine.'

'I hope he is,' Sally said heavily, 'or poor James is going to have even more to cope with than he does already. And he's in a pretty sorry state.'

She'd stayed with him in A and E while Jack had checked him over and she'd stayed with him when his parents had arrived, full of relief and self-recrimination.

And there was no doubt in Sally's mind that they loved James very much indeed.

'Why couldn't he have run away somewhere flat and boring?' Jack said. 'Why did he have to go halfway up a mountain in a howling gale?'

'He was upset,' Sally muttered, 'and you can hardly blame the kid for that.'

She desperately hoped that Lester pulled through or that would be something else for James to deal with.

Wondering why life had to be so complicated, Sally left the A and E department and went back upstairs to the relatives' room on the paediatric ward where she knew Lester's parents were waiting, along with James and his parents.

They were sitting in a huddle, four untouched cups of coffee on the table in front of them.

The moment she entered they looked up anxiously, and Lester's father rose to his feet.

'Any news?'

'Nothing yet,' Sally said gently, 'but they'll tell you as soon as they can.'

'It's all my fault.' James gave a sob and his mother made a distressed sound and pulled him into her arms.

'No, it isn't,' she said firmly. 'If it's anyone's fault it's mine for not telling you sooner, or not telling you in a different way. I did it all wrong.'

But she wasn't doing it wrong now.

Sally felt a lump build in her throat as she watched the woman cuddle the sobbing boy.

She was protecting him through something unpleasant. Wasn't that what mothers were supposed to do?

Suddenly she badly needed to be on her own.

The whole incident had forced her to confront feelings that she'd buried for years, and she felt something catch in her chest.

Satisfied that her presence wasn't needed and finding it all too difficult, she left the room silently and promptly bumped into Tom in the corridor.

'He's fine,' he said quietly, his eyes searching her pale face. 'I've just spoken to the surgical team. They've glued the spleen and checked him over. He'll be in hospital for a few days, but he's doing well.'

'That's good news.' Sally managed a smile, genuinely relieved that the episode had a happy ending. 'Go in and tell them.'

She went to move away from him but he caught her arm. 'Sal...'

He knew.

He knew how she was feeling, just as he always had. 'Not now, Tom.'

She dragged her arm away from his and walked down the corridor as fast as she could, determined not to make a fool of herself in front of him.

If there was one thing she'd learned over her lifetime it was that she could survive on her own.

And she knew that because she'd had to.

Tom cursed silently, watching with a sense of frustration as she hurried away down the corridor.

He knew that the incident had disturbed her and he understood why.

To help save James, she'd delved deep inside herself and bared wounds that she usually kept deeply buried.

And now she'd exposed them.

And she was hurting.

He shifted slightly, feeling her pain as acutely as if it had been his own.

Torn between his desire to go after her and the knowledge that Lester's family was waiting for news in an agony of trepidation, his duties as a doctor won and he forced himself to turn and walk towards the relatives' room.

He'd talk to the family, take them to the intensive care unit to see their son and then he was going after Sally.

And he wasn't going to let her shut him out.

She was emotionally and physically exhausted.

Her bed beckoned, but her mind was too fretful and active to even think about sleeping and she didn't want to lie still and allow her thoughts to overwhelm her.

She needed to keep busy.

Deciding that the answer was to start packing up her

things, ready to move into her new flat the following weekend, she reached for some boxes that she'd put aside ready for that task.

She was halfway through filling the second box when she heard the throaty roar of a motorbike, followed by the sound of footsteps outside the front door.

She froze and stopped breathing for a moment.

It was Tom.

It could only be Tom and he was the last person she wanted to see at the moment.

She didn't want company.

She just wanted to be on her own.

Judging from the impatient thump on the door, he had no intention of respecting that.

She stood still, determined not to answer, assuring herself that he couldn't force her to answer the door.

Finally she heard the roar of the motorbike again and allowed herself to relax, ruthlessly quashing the tiny kernel of disappointment that hovered inside her.

What would have been the point of letting him in?

She didn't intend to lean on Tom.

Sally went back to her packing but in a relatively short time the bike was back again. Her heart thumping, she waited for more knocking but this time all she heard was the sound of a key turning in the door.

Before she had time to wonder how he'd managed to get a key, he'd let himself into the cottage and pushed open the living-room door, his wide shoulders dominating the room.

'What's the matter?' She took one look at his tense features and the recriminations died on her lips. Instead, she scrambled to her feet, concern in her eyes. 'Is something wrong?'

He stopped dead and let out a long breath. 'Not now.'

She stared at him, heart pounding, palms damp. 'What do you mean, not now? What are you doing here? And since when did you have a key?'

'Since I bullied one out of my sister. You wouldn't answer the door. I needed to see if you were OK.' He raked long fingers through his dark hair and dropped his helmet onto the sofa. 'Damn. You gave me a nasty moment.'

It would be so easy to convince herself that he cared. That he—

She pulled herself together, her expression cool and unwelcoming. 'I didn't answer the door because I wanted to be on my own. And I'm not your responsibility, Tom.'

His eyes burned into hers, fire melting the ice. 'What if I said that I want you to be my responsibility.'

Her heart rate doubled. 'I'd say you'd gone mad.'

He wasn't playing fair.

He'd lost the right to say things like that to her a long time ago.

'Maybe I have gone mad.' His voice was rough and he unzipped his leather jacket in a violent movement. 'Or maybe I was mad seven years ago when I let you go.'

The tension in the air was suddenly so charged that she couldn't breathe.

'I don't want to do this, Tom. I can't talk about it now.' Her voice was little more than a whisper. 'I haven't had any sleep and I'm tired.'

'And you're upset over that boy last night.' His eyes raked her tense features. 'Did you think I didn't know? Did you think that I could hear you talking about all those things and not know how badly you were hurting? Or did you just think that I wouldn't care?'

She looked away from him, and pressed a hand to her chest. 'I mean it, Tom. I can't do this—not now. It isn't the right time.'

'Now is precisely the right time.' Tom stepped towards her and placed his hands on her shoulders. 'Because you're vulnerable, and when you're vulnerable I see the real Sally.'

She could feel the strong bite of his fingers through the thin wool of her jumper. 'You're suggesting that I'm not real?'

He was so close that she could hardly breathe and she felt a shiver of sexual awareness spread through her body.

He gave a humourless laugh and this time his hands came up to cup her face. 'Oh, you're real, Sally.' His voice was husky as he tilted her face so that she was forced to look at him.

His mouth hovered only inches from hers and suddenly she forgot why it was that she was supposed to stay away from him.

Why would any woman want to stay away from a man as irresistibly sexy as Tom?

As if she were drugged, she stared up at him, her mind and her senses clouded by the overwhelming attraction between them.

And then his mouth came down on hers, his kiss hard and demanding.

There was no question of resisting him.

Why would she resist something that she wanted so badly? Needed so badly?

Their mouths locked in a wild frenzy, a desperate mating that was almost savage in its intensity. Responding to the building fire in her body, Sally pushed the leather jacket away from his broad shoulders and tugged at his jumper.

Without lifting his mouth from hers, he helped her, shedding the jacket with a rough movement and shuddering as he felt the warmth of her hands slide up his back.

Dragging his mouth from hers with an effort, he ripped off his jumper and then brought his mouth down on hers again and backed her against the wall of the living room.

A lamp smashed to the floor but remained unnoticed.

She could feel him hard and heavy against her and she tried to tell him that he felt good, but her body was no longer under her control and the words wouldn't come.

His mouth seduced hers relentlessly while his hands stripped her roughly, first of her cardigan and lacy bra and finally of her jeans.

'Do you know how badly I've wanted this?' He lifted his mouth from hers just enough to growl the words that needed to be said. Those clever hands slid inside the delicate silk of her panties and dispensed with them swiftly. 'Wanted you?'

Her breath was coming in pants and her body throbbed with a sexual heat so intense that it threatened to overwhelm her. From somewhere she found her voice. 'I want you, too. Now, Tom...'

She dragged his mouth back down to hers, desperate for his kiss, frantic at being denied what she needed so badly. He obliged instantly, his mouth plundering hers while both of them fumbled to remove the rest of his clothing.

There was the sound of tearing that both of them ignored and then finally he was naked and he felt good, *so good*. She sank her teeth into the slick muscle of his shoulder, pulled him closer and felt him, hard and male, pulsing against her. Her body was aching and throbbing and she gave a sob of desperation, pressing closer, raking her nails down his back until he swore softly and lifted her, his hands sliding over the curve of her buttocks as he supported her weight.

Their breath mingled in desperate pants and he adjusted her position and then sheathed himself inside her in an almost primitive act of masculine possession. She cried out in the most exquisite pleasure, her head tipped back and her eyes closed as he thrust again, the pressure of his body pushing her hard against the wall.

But she didn't care.

She welcomed the roughness, the desperation because she felt it, too. That same raw urgency that seemed to devour him engulfed her and consumed her, driving her higher and higher, beyond the limits of human control.

Her whole body shimmered with ferocious sexual need and she wrapped her legs around him, encouraging him, her sobs and gasps intensifying as he drove into her again and again, his body slick and hard against hers.

It had been so long and their need for each other was so great that it couldn't last.

She felt the build of pressure, the sudden increase in masculine thrust and surge of power and then their bodies exploded together in a wild, out-of-control climax that left them both breathless and wordless and shaking with reaction.

Feeling the race of his heart and the harsh sound of his breathing, Sally closed her eyes, overwhelmed by the sensations that still coursed through her trembling body, proof that such a powerful explosion couldn't just vanish into nothing. She swallowed in disbelief as he lowered her gently to the floor, his arms still locked around her.

For endless seconds neither of them spoke, the only sound their fractured breathing and frantic attempts to regain some sort of control.

And then he slid a hand behind her neck and his tone was both rough and gentle at the same time. 'So—if I said I'd missed you, would you believe me?'

There was no missing the humour and irony in his voice and she gave a small smile.

She wanted to say that she'd missed him, too. *That she loved him.*

The thought almost shattered her control.

No, no, no!

She couldn't do this a second time.

She reminded herself that making a mistake once was forgivable, but making the same one twice was nothing short of foolish.

Last time he'd made the decision for both of them.

He was quite capable of doing the same thing again.

Suddenly she needed to minimize what had happened between them. Needed to reduce the shattering impact of his lovemaking.

'I think we both had a stressful day.'

He was silent for a moment and his breathing gradually slowed. 'I've had plenty of stressful days before,' he murmured roughly, lowering his head and branding the soft hollow of her throat with the heat of his mouth, 'but I can assure you that I don't do this.'

She closed her eyes and breathed deeply, steeling herself to reject the affection. *The intimacy.*

She couldn't afford to enjoy it. Couldn't afford to accept it.

With a supreme effort of will, she slid away from him

and stooped to retrieve her cardigan, glancing ruefully at the buttons.

'We always were in too much of a hurry.'

'And why was that?'

He should have looked ridiculous, standing there naked, but he didn't. He looked magnificent. Staggeringly male and shockingly sexy. It was all she could do not to reach for him again and satisfy the craving of her body.

But she couldn't afford to do that.

Tom had all the qualities of an addictive substance. Lethally attractive and dangerous in equal quantities.

And she was going to resist him.

No matter how her body throbbed or her heart ached, she was going to resist him.

'We're both passionate people, Tom. These things happen.'

'Do they?' His gaze burned into hers and he reached for his jeans, dragging them on in a lithe movement. 'You often have mindless sex without even bothering to remove your clothes?'

Her gaze slid pointedly to the untidy pile of clothing remaining on the floor. 'We removed our clothes.'

'Don't do this, Sally. Don't reduce this to nothing.' He yanked up his zip and in two strides he was in front of her, his hands on her arms. 'Have you done that with anyone else?'

She tore her greedy gaze away from the perfect musculature of his chest, determined not to follow the tantalizing line of dark hair that trailed down his taut abdomen.

'My sex life is none of your business, Tom.'

In truth she didn't have a sex life, but there was no

way she was sharing that information with him. It would reveal far too much about herself.

'You're saying this was just sex?'

No. It had been an expression of everything she was. Everything she felt for him.

'Let's not analyse it, Tom.' She pulled away from him before she did something she'd regret. *Said something she'd regret.* 'I'll make you a coffee before you go.'

'That's it?' His tone was incredulous and his blue eyes raked her pale face with ill-disguised frustration. 'We have white-hot sex against the wall *and you offer to make me a coffee before I leave*? What the hell is going on here, Sally?'

Self-protection. That was what was going on.

She looked at him, struggling to keep her expression neutral. 'What do you want?'

'I want you.'

His words pierced her heart more effectively than the sharpest weapon.

'You just had me, Tom.'

His jaw tightened and he inhaled sharply. 'That isn't what I meant, and you know it.'

'I'm not a commodity, Tom. You can't put me down and then expect to pick me up again when it suits you. Last time you wanted me I gave myself to you. I gave every part of myself.' Her voice shook with passion as she spoke the words that she'd been too shattered to speak seven years before. 'I held nothing back. Do you know what it's like to give like that? Because I didn't until I met you. I'd never trusted *anyone* with what I gave you.'

He flinched, guilt flaring in his gaze. 'Sally…'

She nodded, her green eyes flashing sparks and her chin lifting with dignity. 'And you rejected it. I'm an adult woman, Tom, and I have a right to give or with-hold as I choose. I enjoyed the sex. But that's all it was. And now what I want more than anything is to be by myself.'

'No.' He shook his head, his hard jaw set in a deter-mined line. 'That isn't what you want, and we both know it. You were hurt tonight. Do you think I didn't know? When that boy was talking about not having a family, did you think I didn't know what that did to you? I want you to share that with me. I want to be there for you. Talk to me, Sally.'

The addiction was pressing in on her, temptation tak-ing the shape of comfort.

But she recognized it for what it was.

Short-term relief that would bring long-term pain.

She couldn't afford to give any more of herself to this man. So she fought hard against the temptation, deter-mined not to yield. Determined not to be that weak.

If she allowed herself to need him, she made herself vulnerable.

This time when she spoke, her voice was steady. 'Do you have time for a coffee before you leave?'

He swore under his breath and she saw the tiny muscle work in his lean cheek, a sure sign of the pressure he was under. 'Don't pretend it's gone, Sally.' His voice was rough. 'What we have is so powerful that it's going to exist whatever we do. It's always existed. Do you know how hard I struggled to keep my hands off you until you were eighteen?'

Oh, yes, she knew. She'd worked extremely hard to make sure that his struggle was monumental.

She gave a tiny smile that was wholly feminine. 'I seem to recall that I didn't want you to wait.'

'Well, fortunately, seducing a schoolgirl was one

crime I managed not to commit,' he muttered, rubbing a hand over the back of his neck in an effort to relieve the tension. 'But I was always aware that I was the first relationship you'd ever had. In every sense of the word. You had no parents, no one who had ever given you a home. I always worried that you needed more.'

'For me it was never about variety,' she said coolly, 'just about being with the right person. You were that person, Tom. All I ever needed was you. All I ever wanted was you. Unfortunately you didn't feel the same way.'

'I did feel the same way.' His voice was a low growl. 'But I was older than you. I wasn't sure about your feelings. I felt a huge responsibility...' He closed his eyes and his voice was hoarse. 'I made a mistake, Sally, and if I could have my time again I'd do things differently. I'd be totally selfish. Lock you away and keep you for myself. But it isn't too late.'

'It's too late for me.'

'Is it?' His voice was velvety soft and disturbingly male. 'So have you found it again, Sally? The love that we share? Have you found it with anyone else?'

She could barely find her voice. 'Shared. What we had is in the past tense, Tom.'

It had to be.

She couldn't risk the same thing happening a second time.

'Our love will never be in the past tense, and that's what makes it special. No matter what we do, no matter what mistakes we make, it will always be there. It will always be pulling us together. Why do you think I'm not married, Sally?'

'I really don't—'

'Because no other woman is you, and no other woman

ever can be. And I'm going to make you trust me again if it takes the rest of my life to achieve it.'

She stood frozen to the spot, wishing he'd leave before she cracked and decided that the short-term pleasure was worth the price of long-term pain. 'It won't happen, Tom.'

'It's going to happen.' His mouth came down on hers with a sense of purpose, his tongue dipping and coaxing in a slow seduction that was every bit as erotic as the fiery heat had been. 'Can you live without this, Sally?' His hand curved around her cheek and his eyes were half-closed as he kissed her, tasted her. 'Without this you're living your life in black and white, not colour. Is that what you want?'

She flinched and backed away, feeling the slow build of desire engulf her body again. 'Sometimes colour blinds you to the true state of the world.'

'Marry me, Sally.' His voice was hoarse and urgent. 'Marry me and we'll be the family you always wanted us to be.'

Marry him?

His words drove the breath from her body and for a moment she swayed, drawn by the memories and the look in his eyes.

And then she remembered that this man was capable of breaking her heart and she wasn't so foolish that she believed that marriage would protect her. Marriages ended.

If he'd let her go before, he could let her go again.

She drew in a breath. 'I take it you don't want coffee.' She moved towards the door, ignoring her shaking legs and her thumping heart. 'I'll see you out.'

There was a tense, throbbing silence and then she

heard the sound of him dragging on the rest of his clothes.

She didn't look back.

By the time he joined her in the hallway she had the front door open. Freezing cold air flowed through the doorway, reminding her that heat and warmth couldn't last.

He paused in the doorway, his black helmet under his arm. His leathers accentuated the width of his shoulders and the strength of his thighs, and she felt the need explode inside her again.

The truth was that the passion between them was a living, breathing force. More powerful than both of them.

She could put oceans between them but she'd never be free of him.

This need that consumed her would be with her for ever.

'You're going to say yes, Sally.' His voice was soft and loaded with purpose, and before she could protest or resist he brought his mouth down on hers again, intensifying the reaction that the mere sight of his body had already started. His warm mouth seduced hers and then he lifted his head reluctantly. 'If I have to ask you every day for the rest of our lives, you're going to say yes.'

Without giving her time to reply, he pushed the helmet onto his head and strode over to his bike.

Tom let himself into the converted barn that had been his home for the past five years. He dropped his keys on the table and immediately poured himself a large whiskey.

Despite the almost animal urgency of their lovemaking, his whole body was still throbbing with unfulfilled need.

As far as he was concerned, that had only been a starter.

Given his way, he'd have carried her upstairs and carried on where they'd left off for the rest of the night.

He ran a hand over the back of his neck, sweat breaking out on his brow as he remembered the wildness and the desperation.

They'd both lost control.

Had he hurt her?

Guilt and concern rippled through him, but then he reached for his glass and felt the sting of the wounds she'd inflicted with her teeth and nails. He gave a totally masculine smile and lifted a hand to his shoulder, remembering how she'd met him bite for bite, comforted by the evidence that she'd wanted him every bit as desperately as he'd wanted her.

She'd burned for him as he'd burned for her.

No matter how much she denied it, how much she fought it, they were meant to be together.

He should have realized that seven years ago. But he hadn't been able to trust that what she'd felt for him had been real.

But now he knew that it was more real than anything else in his life.

And being with Sally mattered more than anything else in his life.

He sucked in a breath and finished his whiskey, facing the indisputable fact that she was going to fight him. That she was determined to not allow herself to be hurt a second time.

It was going to be hard to persuade her that loving him didn't present a risk.

Even harder to persuade her to trust him enough to marry him.

He stood still, a frown creasing his brow, deep in thought. And then the solution came to him and a smile spread across his face.

She thought that she could live without him. Live without what they'd shared tonight.

It was up to him to show her that she couldn't.

CHAPTER EIGHT

IF SALLY had thought working with Tom had been difficult before they'd made love, afterwards it became almost intolerable.

Every time he walked onto the unit she dropped something, and she found it almost impossible to concentrate on what he was saying. Instead, she saw the power of his shoulders and the gleam in his eyes. And the heat of his gaze was a constant reminder of the frantic, out-of-control passion that they'd shared in the cottage.

Even without the broken lamp for evidence, she wouldn't have been able to forget it.

Memories of the encounter simmered in both her mind and her body, denting her concentration and threatening her willpower.

There was an ache inside her that wouldn't be subdued. A need that pulsed quietly, threatening to engulf her. She gritted her teeth, telling herself that such a reaction was to be expected. She hadn't slept with a man since Tom. Hadn't wanted to. But now her body had been reawakened and it refused to return to its previously dormant state.

She told herself that she'd lived without Tom for seven years. Survived. But she was learning that there was a huge difference between survival and fulfilment.

Dragging her mind back to the job, she concentrated on the labouring woman she'd been attending all morning.

It had all the signs of being a perfectly straightforward

delivery, which was a good thing. At least Tom wouldn't get involved.

Trying hard not to think about him, she glanced up as the door opened.

One of the student midwives stood there, a look of panic on her face. 'Sister needs you in Room 2.'

Calmly Sally stood up. 'That's fine, Alice. I'll go to her. Will you stay with Mrs Jones for me, please?'

Without asking for any further information, she quickly made her apologies to the woman she'd been with all morning and slipped out onto the unit.

Immediately she picked up the tension and took a step backwards as an anaesthetist that she knew vaguely sprinted down the corridor towards Theatre, almost knocking her sideways.

She hurried to Room 2, opened the door and then stopped as she saw Tom.

But he wasn't looking at her.

His expression was grim and his handsome face reflected the tension that pulsed in the room.

'Raise the foot of the bed and keep that head pushed back, Emma. I don't need to tell you not to handle the cord or it might go into spasm.'

Realizing immediately that they were dealing with a prolapsed cord, Sally moved towards the bed, helping to elevate it.

'What can I do?'

Emma was using her fingers to prevent the baby's head from pressing down on the cord and cutting off the blood supply from the placenta. Sally knew that she wouldn't be able to remove her hand until the baby was safely delivered.

If it was safely delivered.

Cord compression was an emergency and a cause of foetal death.

Tom glanced at her, his expression urgent. 'Help me get Lynne on her hands and knees. I want her bottom higher than her head. Then I want to infuse 500 mils of saline into her bladder. She isn't fully dilated. I'm going to section her.'

They worked together swiftly and then, satisfied that the mother was in the best possible position, Tom strode towards the door. 'Get her into Theatre and make sure she's breathing one hundred per cent oxygen. I'll go and scrub.'

The door swung closed behind him and Sally looked at Emma for an explanation.

'This is Lynne. It's her third baby. Her waters broke this morning but we seem to have a shoulder presentation and the cord has prolapsed.'

'Are you OK?' Sally mouthed the question, knowing that maintaining the necessary pressure on the baby's head must be tiring for Emma. Her colleague gave a brief nod.

'Yes,' she replied softly. 'But we need to get her into Theatre.'

'I'll scrub and assist.'

At that moment several other people hurried into the room to help, and together they wheeled Lynne through to Theatre.

Her husband followed and hovered in the corridor, white-faced and breathing rapidly.

Sally paused. 'Come with us,' she said gently. 'You can wait in the recovery room next to Theatre.'

She showed him where to go and then hurried through to Theatre and scrubbed.

Tom was already gowned and masked and waiting

for the patient. 'Someone get a paediatrician down here—now.'

One of the other midwives hurried to make the call and Tom turned his attention back to the patient.

'Hurry up,' he growled at the anaesthetist, who gave a nod of understanding.

'I'm ready when you are. Carry on.'

There were few other obstetric emergencies where speed was so vital. The whole team understood the urgency and the usual cheerful buzz of the theatre was replaced by virtual silence.

Working like clockwork and with no verbal communication necessary, Sally handed him the instruments he needed at the exact time he needed them, and Tom performed the fastest, slickest Caesarean she'd ever witnessed.

His fingers were swift and sure, using the scalpel to stroke through the layers of skin and muscle to expose the lower segment of the uterus.

Sally watched in awe as he made a small, transverse incision with the scalpel and then widened it with his fingers. Then he passed his right hand into the uterus and lifted the baby's head, instructing his registrar to press on the fundus to push the baby out. After a few tense seconds, during which no one watching breathed or moved, he manoeuvred the baby out and into the waiting hands of the paediatrician.

There was no cry and Sally felt her heart lurch.

Were they too late?

Despite the speed with which Tom had acted, had the baby's oxygen supply been cut off by pressure on the cord?

Tom still had his hands in the uterus, delivering the placenta, but his eyes lifted once to the corner of the room where the paediatrician was leaning over the rescusitaire.

'Give me some news on that baby. And make it good news.' His voice was hoarse and reflected the concern and urgency that they all felt.

And then suddenly there was a thin, reedy cry that turned into a furious yell.

A smile spread across Sally's face and she looked at Tom, her eyes filled with tears.

'Have I ever told you you're brilliant?'

He closed his eyes for a moment and she felt the tension ooze out of him, saw his wide shoulders sag slightly. Then he opened them again and they gleamed above his mask.

'I think you should be praising Emma. She's the one with cramp in her right hand.'

Emma smiled and waggled her fingers ruefully. 'I always find normal deliveries so boring,' she quipped, and Tom rolled his eyes.

'You midwives are never satisfied. Can we do a swab count before I close?'

Looking at the hint of dark stubble on his hard jaw and the thickness of his dark lashes, Sally felt her heart kick against her chest and a pulsing warmth spread through her body.

He was an incredible doctor.

And an incredible man.

And, like it or not, she was stuck loving him for the rest of her life.

Suddenly she wanted him so badly it was a physical ache. She needed him. She might not be prepared to risk her heart, but there was nothing stopping her enjoying a physical relationship with him, was there?

Watching his strong, clever fingers skilfully stitching

Lynne's uterus, she suddenly wanted him so much that her vision blurred and she felt dizzy.

'Are you all right?' His deep voice was concerned and she lifted her eyes to his.

And he saw.

His blue gaze locked on hers and held her captive while he read everything that was in her thoughts.

And then he smiled and nodded. A confident, satisfied smile.

The smile of a male who knew he had the upper hand.

Bother.

She handed him another suture, her body humming with a sexual anticipation so powerful that she was amazed the other people in the theatre couldn't feel it.

The tension between them was electric, intensified by the drama of the life-threatening situation they'd just been involved in.

Why shouldn't she relieve that tension?

Why shouldn't she enjoy a physical relationship with the man?

Breathlessly conscious of every masculine inch of him, her eyes clung to his forearms and worked upwards over the smooth swell of his biceps.

Clashing with the heat in his blue gaze, she dragged her eyes back to the wound, watching while he worked.

Finally the wound was closed and Lynne was transferred to the recovery room.

Emma went with her and the paediatrician followed with the baby, who was pronounced totally fit and well.

Hideously conscious of Tom watching her, Sally ripped off her gloves and her mask and started to clear up.

'My office.' His voice came from immediately behind

her and the raw need in his tone made her gasp. 'Five minutes.'

She opened her mouth to refuse but no sound came out. And he didn't hang around to give her time to protest.

Instead, he strode out of Theatre without a backward glance, leaving every bone in her body aching with longing.

She gave a start as Emma came back into the room. 'Alice is with Lynne. She's doing well. Isn't Tom brilliant? He tries so hard not to section women that you wonder whether he even knows how to do it, and then there's an emergency like that and—bam!' She slammed her hand into her fist and grinned. 'He's so confident and competent that it makes you drool, doesn't it?'

Sally stood still, struggling to control her own reaction to Tom. She was trying very hard not to drool. 'He's very good.'

'Good? The man's a genius.' Emma gave a wistful sigh. 'Can you imagine what the man must be like in bed?'

Sally closed her eyes briefly.

She knew exactly what he was like in bed.

'He wants to see me in his office, Emma,' she said, wondering if Emma would detect the slightly husky note in her voice. But the other woman just looked surprised.

'I wonder why? Probably to tell you that you did a good job in a crisis. He's very good at praising people. And you were brilliant, Sally. You just got stuck in without asking any questions.'

Sally smiled and moved towards the door. 'I think you were the one who was stuck in.'

'Don't!' Emma laughed. 'I'm going to have a cramp

in my right hand for the rest of the day. Go on. If he
wants to see you, you'd better shift.'

Tom stood in his office, staring out of the window, wondering how long he'd have to wait.

His body hummed with a sexual tension so powerful
that it was almost painful, and when he heard the soft
tap on the door he felt a rush of anticipation.

Quickly he gritted his teeth and reminded himself of
his plan.

'You wanted me?' Sally's voice was smoky and soft
and he knew that she'd phrased the question in that particular way by design, not accident.

He turned, noticing the heightened colour of her
cheeks and the brightness of her green eyes.

Her blonde hair shone under the harsh light of his
office and she was still wearing a scrub suit that showed
off the curves that he knew so intimately.

*And he wanted her more than he'd ever wanted a
woman in his life.*

'Marry me, Sally.'

He saw the soft look in her eyes turn to shock and
then wariness.

'Tom, for goodness' sake…'

He closed the distance between them, his eyes never
leaving hers. 'Marry me.'

She shook her head and backed towards the door, but
he slid an arm round her waist and hauled her against
him, using the other to turn the key and ensure that they
weren't disturbed.

'I don't even want to have this conversation.'

But the scrub suit was made of thin cotton and he felt
the power of her response to him, saw her nipples peak
under the revealing fabric, saw the confusion in her eyes.

'Fine.' He lowered his head, his mouth hovering only a breath away from hers. 'No conversation.'

And then he kissed her.

She tasted fantastic and he groaned against her mouth, his lips and tongue exploring her intimately, stoking the fire that was already burning inside both of them.

He held her hard against him with one hand, feeling the softness of her body through the almost non-existent barrier of her scrub suit. The other hand he slid upwards, cupping her breast and teasing her nipple with the tips of his fingers.

She sucked in her breath and detached her lips from his, but he lifted his hand and slid it into her hair, bringing her mouth back to his with determined force.

Desire throbbed inside him and he felt her instant response, felt her press against him, felt the moment she yielded.

Her hands slid around him, pulling him closer, and her mouth opened under his, allowing him access.

He took full advantage, tasting and teasing until he felt her fingers biting into the muscle of his shoulders, felt her need rise up to meet his.

And that was when he pulled away.

For a moment she swayed, then she stared at him dizzily, her expression devoid of comprehension.

He drew in a breath that was decidedly unsteady and struggled to resist the temptation of her soft mouth. 'Marry me.'

She looked at him blankly, her lips parted, her eyes still clouded with passion. 'Tom?'

He slid a hand under her chin and stared down into her face, thinking that she was the most beautiful woman he'd ever seen in his life. 'I said, marry me.'

She closed her eyes and reached for him again, but

he took a step backwards, shaking his head, wondering which one of them he was torturing the most.

'No. Not again.' Ignoring the almost agonizing throb of his body, he denied himself. Denied both of them. 'Not until we're married.'

This time he had her attention.

Wide, startled green eyes fixed on his. 'You cannot possibly be serious.'

'I've never been more serious in my life. I know I hurt you, Sally, and I regret that more than you will ever know, but I'm going to make it up to you.'

She shook her head and stood staring at him, her fists clenched by her sides, her knuckles white. 'No.'

His eyes searched hers and he saw the pain and confusion. 'I want you to trust me, Sally, and I'm going to show you that you can.'

Her chin lifted. 'No.'

Her strength and determination was amazing and he was just thankful that his determination exceeded hers.

She was going to marry him.

He played his final card and brought his mouth down on hers again, the kiss brief but devastating.

The flames licked and burned, and when he lifted his head his voice was rough with barely restrained passion. 'Can you live without it, Sally? Can you honestly live without what we have?'

'What we share is physical.' She gave what she obviously thought was a casual shrug, but it didn't convince either of them. 'I'm prepared to have an affair.'

'That's not enough. And, Sally…' He spoke the words softly. 'What we share is love.'

She stared at him for a long moment, denial and confusion in her eyes, and then she turned and fumbled with the key, unlocking his office door and almost stumbling in her speed to get away from him.

He stopped himself from going after her, taking comfort from the fact that he'd never expected to win the war with the first battle.

His plan was only just beginning.

Love?

Sally stood in the toilet and took several deep breaths.

Her body was screaming with a sexual frustration that she hadn't known she was capable of feeling, and she leaned her head against the wall and cursed Tom.

How dared he?

How dared he use the passion between them to push for something more when he knew she wasn't willing to take that risk?

The man was so arrogant!

She straightened up and stared at herself in the mirror, her green eyes flashing fire.

He obviously believed that she couldn't live without him.

Without his touch.

For a brief moment her body tingled, but she clenched her fists and forced herself to ignore the sensation.

She'd lived without Tom's touch, without his love, for seven long years. She could do it again.

But that had been before she'd been given a taste of what she was missing.

Memories of that night in the cottage flooded through her and she gave a groan of denial, wishing now that it had never happened.

It would have been so much easier to turn her back on something that was only a distant memory. But to reject a passion that was so fierce, *so alive*, was almost asking the impossible.

Almost, but not quite.

Turning on the cold tap, she leaned forward and splashed her face, feeling the water cool her flushed cheeks.

She couldn't give her love to him again. Couldn't risk the rejection that had almost destroyed her seven years before.

She wouldn't make herself that vulnerable again.

She was going to resist him.

But it was easier said than done.

Wherever she was, Tom seemed to be there.

Even when she was doing a normal delivery that had no need for the presence of an obstetrician, he seemed to find a reason to pop in and ask her something.

And their awareness of each other was rising to such an intensity that Sally could hardly breathe.

Even in her social life there was no escape. If she went for a drink with the mountain rescue team, he was there. If she went for supper with Bryony and Jack, he was there.

Even when she spent an evening at Helen's, discussing the wedding, he was there, sharing a beer with Oliver.

Finally she cornered Bryony at the final fitting of their bridesmaids' dresses.

'The wedding's on Saturday,' Bryony said cheerfully, doing a twirl and trying to see her back in the mirror. 'If they don't fit now, we're in trouble.'

'They fit beautifully,' Helen said, smiling from the depths of a comfortable sofa. 'Try them with the shoes.'

Sally winced. 'I don't think I can walk in those shoes.'

Helen laughed. 'I'll give you lessons. And if you struggle you can always hold Tom's arm. He is the best man after all.'

Sally gritted her teeth. She didn't need reminding that he was the best man. Oliver and Helen's wedding was just another occasion where she was going to have to avoid him.

Twice during the day he'd cornered her.

Twice he'd kissed her until her body had been one big screaming ache.

And then he'd walked away.

If she hadn't seen the tension in his wide shoulders and heard the uncharacteristic snap in his voice when he spoke, she'd have thought that he was finding the whole thing amusing.

But there was no laughter in those sexy blue eyes.

Only determination.

And a raw masculine need that almost took her breath away.

'He loves you, Sally.' Bryony spoke in a quiet voice and she and Helen exchanged glances. 'And you know you love him.'

Sally adjusted the neck of her dress. 'Do you think this is too revealing?'

Bryony frowned. 'Sally…'

'Look.' Sally turned to face her, her breathing rapid. 'I don't want to talk about this, all right? I really, *really* don't want to talk about it.'

As far as she was concerned, it was a problem that couldn't be solved by talking so she wanted to just try to ignore it.

Eventually it would go away.

It had to.

'I was angry with him, too, you know that,' Bryony

said quietly, 'but he thought he was doing the right thing and he regrets it so much, Sally. I've never seen my brother doubt himself before—never seen him admit that he was wrong, but he's admitting it now. He used to be everything to you. Can't you forgive him?'

Sally paused. 'Yes, I can forgive him.' She stared at her reflection in the mirror, thankful that the glass only reflected what was on the outside. *If people could see what was going on inside, she'd be in big trouble.* 'But I can't let him be everything to me any more. I can't take that chance.'

Bryony opened her mouth again but Helen lifted a hand to silence her and stood up.

'Surely love always means taking a chance,' she said quietly. 'There are never any guarantees for any one of us. All we can do is make the best decision we can at the time and take any chance of happiness that comes our way.'

Sally's face was stony. 'And learn from our mistakes.'

'But what if Tom has learned from his?' Helen's voice was soft. 'What if he truly does believe that he was wrong? Are you going to risk letting that chance of happiness slip away?' She gave a rueful smile. 'Look at me. Oliver asked me to marry him within about three seconds of meeting him. I just couldn't believe that he could possibly mean it. How could I trust that something so new could last?'

Sally stared at her. 'So why did you?'

Helen gave a soft smile. 'Because the alternative— losing Oliver—was more than I could bear. Tom made a mistake, Sally, but, if anything, that mistake will make your relationship stronger. Everyone can see how much he loves you and how much you love him. He's a proud guy and yet he's willing to humble himself in public in his attempt to persuade you to forgive him. That's got to tell you something about the way he feels. Take a leap of faith.'

Sally was silent, her fingers playing with the silky fabric of her dress. 'I don't think I can do that.'

It was asking too much.

Bryony gave a short laugh and exchanged a satisfied glance with Helen. 'Well, if you're not going to, you'd better brace yourself for a siege,' she said lightly, 'because, judging from the set of his shoulders, my brother isn't about to take no for an answer.'

The next day Sally walked into the storeroom to collect some equipment and gave a soft gasp as Tom walked in behind her and closed the door.

The room was small and presented absolutely no opportunities for escape.

There was no need for build-up.

The sexual tension between them had reached flash point.

Taking refuge in defence, she gritted her teeth and glared at him. 'Don't you have anything better to do than corner me in the storeroom? You're becoming boring, Tom.'

And she wanted him so badly the ache was becoming intolerable.

His firm mouth curved into a smile. 'Boring?' His voice was husky and very, very male. 'Is that right?' He slid a hand behind her neck and drew her closer.

She felt her knees weaken. 'Tom, for goodness' sake…'

'You look tired.' His mouth hovered wickedly close to hers. 'Are you sleeping at night, sweetheart? Or is something keeping you awake?'

The soft endearment made her heart turn over and she had to bite back the sob of need that rose in her throat.

'I'm sleeping perfectly.'

She wanted him to kiss her.

She needed him to kiss her so badly.

Without even knowing that she was doing it, she rose on tiptoe and tried to close the distance between her mouth and his, but he drew back just enough to prevent the ultimate contact but not enough to ease the frantic throb that tortured her pelvis.

Her body was on fire.

'Marry me, Sally.' His mouth was so close to hers that she could almost taste him and her eyes closed and she swayed towards him.

'Tom, please—'

'Marry me.'

Through the fog of sexual need, a question formed in her brain.

How was it that he was so controlled?

How was he able to resist what she needed so badly?

And then she felt the brush of his arousal through the thin fabric of her scrub suit and realized that he was struggling as much as she was.

The knowledge gave her satisfaction.

'You want marriage, Tom.' Her voice was smoky soft and all temptress. 'And I'm prepared to have an affair. Are you going to refuse that?'

She ran the tip of her tongue over her lower lip and heard his sharp intake of breath, saw his eyes fix hungrily on her mouth.

The atmosphere froze.

And then his mouth claimed hers with a violence that drew a sob of relief from her.

One hand held her head still for his kiss and the other

curved over her bottom, drawing her against him, letting her feel what she did to him.

'Tom…' Frantic with haste, forgetting where they were, she pulled her mouth away from his just enough to gasp his name and then yanked his shirt out of his trousers. Breathing rapidly, she let her fingers slide over the sleek muscle of his back, loving the feel of his body. 'Please, I—'

He brought his mouth back down on hers and she felt his hand slide inside the loose bottoms of her scrub suit, felt the sure, knowing touch of his fingers driving her mindless while his mouth teased and tormented.

She wriggled and arched, the intimacy of his skilled caress releasing an almost intolerable excitement deep within her.

'No…' He groaned the word against her mouth and suddenly she was deprived of both his touch and his kiss.

She leaned towards him, desperate for him to finish what he'd started. Her whole body was throbbing. 'If this is your idea of a joke…'

'Do I look as though I'm laughing?' His breathing was unsteady and all traces of humour had gone from his tone. 'I don't want an affair with you, Sally. It isn't enough. I want everything.'

She stared at him in disbelief, wondering how he could manage conversation when she could barely stand upright. But then she looked closer and saw the lines of tension and the storm in his blue eyes.

He was struggling, too.

'Tom—'

'Marry me.' His voice was hoarse. 'Marry me and I'm going to take you to bed and make love to you until neither of us has the energy to move.'

'I can't marry you.' Her reply was little more than a whisper and she saw his hard jaw tighten.

'I can't do this any more.' His eyes blazed into hers. 'I don't trust myself around you. When you change your mind, come to me. Until then, I'm keeping my distance.'

The day before the wedding the mountain rescue team was called out.

Since their encounter in the storeroom, Sally had spent more sleepless nights and was feeling tense and on edge.

When you change your mind, come to me.

Well, she wasn't going to change her mind.

And she wasn't going to go to him.

She gritted her teeth as she pulled on her warm clothes and prepared for the rescue, facing the fact that she was going to be working shoulder to shoulder with Tom.

She considered asking if she could be partnered with someone else and then decided that a request like that would attract too much unwanted attention from the rest of the team and they were already the subject of considerable speculation.

And a request like that would also let Tom know that his campaign to drive her slowly mad from frustration was working.

And she didn't want him to know.

Didn't want him to know that she couldn't sleep at night because her dreams were haunted by visions of him.

Didn't want him to know that she couldn't concentrate at work because her days were punctuated by tantalizing glimpses of him in the distance.

Didn't want him to know that she could no longer enjoy the mountains or her work on the team because she was so aware of his presence next to her.

Pulling on her jacket and the rest of her gear, she forced herself to concentrate on the briefing.

'A woman's dog has gone over the edge—and she can't see it. She's been wandering for ages, trying to track it down, and now has no idea where she is or where the dog might be.' Sean gave a sigh and shook his head. 'One day someone is going to make it mandatory to learn to use a map and compass before a person sets foot on the fells. OK, folks. We've got a lot of ground to cover. This is the plan.'

He briefed them in detail, using the map, and they set out, dividing up so that they could cover a wider area.

Sally walked briskly in front of Tom, deciding that she'd rather be in front of him than behind him. At least that way she didn't have to look at his broad shoulders and his long legs.

Thanks to his campaign of looking but not touching, her need for him had grown to such a pitch that she was no longer able to be in the same room as him without having indecent thoughts.

'Doesn't matter how fast you walk, Sally, I'll still be right here.'

His voice came from directly behind her and she whirled around, her eyes blazing.

'Stop tormenting me.'

'Why?' One dark eyebrow lifted in gentle mockery. 'If you're indifferent to me, it shouldn't be possible to torment you, and if you're not indifferent…'

She ground her teeth. 'Trust me, I'm indifferent.'

He nodded. 'So what's causing those black shadows under your eyes?' He lifted a hand and stroked a finger down her cheek, smiling slightly as she shivered. 'It's the same thing that's causing the black shadows under mine. And it's called frustration.'

She glared at him. 'And who is responsible for that?'

'You.' He smiled. 'By refusing to marry me.'

'I don't want to marry you.' She voiced the words automatically, but even as she spoke she felt the first flicker of doubt. Then she pulled herself together and lifted her chin, her gaze provocative and challenging. 'I've told you, I just want hot sex with you.'

If she'd expected to shock him, she was disappointed.

He stepped closer to her, his blue eyes trapping hers. 'You can have endless, scorching sex with me—' his voice was a lazy drawl '—once we're married. Just say the word.'

'I'm not that stupid, Tom.' She backed away and shifted the pack on her back. 'And I'm not that desperate.'

She thought she heard him mutter, 'But you will be.' She chose to ignore it, stomping up the path at an increased pace, trying to ease some of her mental and physical frustration through exercise.

An hour later they'd climbed to the top of a ridge and Sally paused. 'According to Sean, this was where the dog went over.' She glanced around and then took several steps over. 'Look—she's left a hat. She obviously panicked and didn't collect all her things. So we're definitely in the right place.'

Tom squinted around, his strong legs braced as he steadied himself against the wind. 'Can't see anything or anyone.'

'Well, if the dog went over there…' Sally peered over the ridge '…then I suppose she would have tried to get down to the bottom, which means she would have taken this path upwards and then down to the right.'

Tom looked at her. 'That's only if she knows the territory as well as you do.'

'If she'd gone straight over the edge, we'd see her body,' Sally said reasonably, 'and the chances are that she approached from the other direction anyway, so she'd know that there's a path that leads down to the bottom.'

Tom nodded. 'OK. Lead on.'

They found the woman crouched on the edge of the path further along, staring into the sharp drop.

As they approached, Sally called out a warning, anxious that their sudden arrival didn't startle the woman.

'You're too close to the edge.' She hurried up to the woman and gently coaxed her away from the precipitous drop.

'She fell.' The woman's face was chalk white and her eyes were full of tears. 'She was bouncing along the path, playing, and suddenly it just fell away. She scrabbled frantically and yelped and then she just disappeared.'

'And she's on a ledge?'

The woman nodded, her lower lip caught between her teeth. 'You probably think I'm crazy, making all this fuss about a dog. But she's all I've got.'

Sally gave her shoulder a squeeze. 'I don't think you're crazy. And we'll get her for you. Just make sure she stays still on that ledge.'

'I'm trying to…' the woman's eyes filled '…but she wants to get back to me and she keeps jumping up.'

'Well, at least she's fit enough to jump,' Sally said practically, taking various bits of equipment from Tom as he removed them from his rucksack.

It occurred to her that in almost every aspect of their lives they worked together almost by telepathy, each responding to an instinctive knowledge of what the other needed.

Reminding herself that she wasn't going to think about what she needed, Sally moved alongside Tom and wriggled into a harness. She clipped on a karabiner and attached the rope.

'I'll abseil down to her,' she said quietly, and Tom nodded, checking the knot on her rope.

'Don't do any of your fancy tricks, Jenner.' His tone was light. 'Just get the dog and leave, got that? No social chit-chat. None of your free climbing or flash moves.'

She smiled mockingly, paying out the rope and stepping towards the edge. 'I might hang around if the view is nice.'

She abseiled skilfully and confidently down the side of the mountain and stopped by the ledge where the little dog was trapped.

As soon as the dog saw her, she started to wag her tail frantically.

Sally saw the danger instantly and gave a gasp of dismay. 'Stay! Sit! Oh, help, you're going to fall, you silly thing.' Seeing the dog's back legs slide off the ledge, she lunged across and grabbed it by the collar, just managing to secure it before it plummeted down to the valley floor.

Her heart was thumping so hard she thought it might explode out of her chest. 'Don't do that to me again,' she scolded, drawing the dog towards her and attaching the harness and the rope. Satisfied that the dog was safely attached, she indicated to Tom that she was ready for him to lift the dog, and then concentrated on climbing back up to them.

Back on the ridge the woman collapsed on the little dog, hugging her tightly.

'I can never thank you enough for saving her. I saw what happened. If you hadn't caught her when you did... She's all I've got.' She buried her face in the dog's coat and closed her eyes.

Sally unfastened the rope. 'Well, I did catch her, so let's not think about it.'

The woman gave a sniff. 'She doesn't even seem injured. She was so lucky to land on that ledge. If she'd gone over...'

Tom put a hand on her arm. 'As Sally said, let's not think about it. Come on. Let's get you off this mountain. The weather is closing in.'

But before they reached the bottom another call came from Sean, reporting four boys overdue from a walk.

They agreed that Tom would rendezvous with the rest of the team and Sally would continue to the bottom and take the woman and the dog safely to base.

Initially relieved to be away from the temptation of being near Tom, Sally glanced at the sky and suddenly felt a twinge of disquiet. There was a storm brewing and it had all the signs of being a bad one.

It would mean a difficult and potentially dangerous rescue for Tom and the rest of the team.

Dragging her eyes away from the building cloud, she concentrated on guiding the woman and her dog to safety.

An hour later she climbed on her bike to ride home from the base and then looked at the weather again and decided to wait.

She wouldn't be able to relax, knowing that Tom was out there.

She needed to be at the heart of what was happening.

And it wasn't as if he ever needed to know that she'd stayed.

Sean was inside, on the radio to Tom and Oliver. 'According to the parents they were headed for the ghyll—

start there.' He glanced up as Sally walked into the room. 'I thought we'd got rid of you.' He lifted an eyebrow in a silent question and she gave a rueful shrug, trying to look casual.

'I thought I might hang around here with you. You're going to need some moral support with the parents. They've just arrived and they look as though they need coffee...' Her voice tailed off under Sean's steady gaze.

'Sally.' His tone was firm as he lounged back in his chair. 'Just marry the man and stop all this messing around.'

Colour touched her cheeks. 'I don't know what you mean.'

He sighed wearily and stabbed his fingers through his cropped dark hair. 'The whole community knows what I mean. At the moment neither you nor Tom have your mind on the job in hand and I don't want distracted people out there on the fells. Sort it out. Say yes to the guy, Sally. Then Tom will stop drinking my whiskey and you'll stop staring at me like a puppy worried that his master won't come home.'

Sally bristled. 'He isn't my master.'

'But you're worried he won't come home.' Sean's gaze fixed on hers. 'Heaven knows, I'm no expert on emotions, but doesn't that tell you anything, Sal? The fact that you're still sitting here in this boring building where nothing is going to happen for hours. Doesn't that tell you something?'

Yes.

But she didn't want to hear it. She wanted to ignore it.

She swallowed, aware that Sean was looking at her expectantly.

She gave a helpless shrug, knowing that denial was a

waste of time. 'All right! I know I love Tom,' she said
finally, 'but I'm scared, Sean. *Really* terrified—and too
scared to risk it all again. Do you have any idea what it
was like? Trying to live without him?'

'Seems to me that you're living without him at the
moment anyway, so how much worse could it get,
Sally?' He let out a long breath and pulled a face. 'Let's
look at it another way. You were the bravest kid I ever
knew. When you were thirteen, Tom and I used to bawl
at you to use a rope, and every time we turned round
you'd be up that rock-face with a grin on your face and
absolutely nothing holding you there except your fingers,
your feet and your incredible determination. What's happened to those guts, Sally?'

Her lips felt stiff. 'I still free climb.'

He nodded. 'I know you do. So that's still one risk
you're prepared to take. What about other risks? Why
are some risks worth taking while others aren't? With
Tom you're too wary to even put a foot on the rock-
face.'

She couldn't answer him, shaken by the analogy that
he'd used.

She'd never thought of herself as a coward.

Sean ran a hand over the back of his neck. 'Why do
you climb?'

'Because I love it. Because I can't not climb.'

'And if you fell one day?' He looked at her. 'Would
you still climb?'

She frowned and then nodded. 'Yes. Of course I
would. It's a part of me. Of who I am.'

'And so is Tom. And that's why you'll never be happy
unless you're with him.' Sean glanced at the clock and
made a move towards the door. 'Enough psychology. It
isn't exactly my forte, but when I see two people I love

making a mess of things, I have to interfere. That's what comes of being married to my wife for so many years. And now I need to talk to the families of those children and you need to spend some time facing up to the truth, Sally. Don't punish him for one mistake. You fell once, but your love for him is still there. You can't live without Tom. He's every bit as much a part of you as your climbing. And at some point you're going to have to get back on that rock-face or you'll have wasted your life by being too afraid to go after the one thing you want.'

He walked quietly out of the room and closed the door behind him, leaving her staring after him in silence, her thoughts clearer than they'd been for a long time.

It was the longest evening of Sally's life and for the first time she understood how it must feel to be a relative with a loved one lost on the mountain.

Tom was a skilled mountaineer and he wasn't lost.

But for some reason she still couldn't stop worrying.

And suddenly she knew Sean was right. Tom was as much a part of her as her climbing. And she couldn't live without him.

Sean was prowling anxiously around the base, and when the radio crackled to life he dived for it, expecting to hear Tom's voice.

It was Oliver, and even though his voice crackled and broke up periodically, they could hear the tension in his voice.

'We've got them. Tom saved one of the boys from going over the edge, but he's fallen and he's got a nasty gash on his leg. It's bleeding like crazy. We need a helicopter.'

Sean swung into action and Sally sank down onto the nearest chair.

She knew that when the wind was this high it was unlikely that a helicopter would be able to take off, let alone land.

In between calls, Sean glanced across at her. 'You're white as a sheet,' he said roughly. 'Go and make yourself a hot drink. And stop worrying about Tom. He's made of stern stuff.'

He went back to his calls and Sally wandered aimlessly around the base, waiting and worrying.

She wanted him safely back.

She wanted to tell him that she loved him.

Finally they had the news that the wind had dropped sufficiently for the helicopter to land and pick up Tom and one of the boys. The other three were well enough to be walked off the mountain by the remaining members of the team.

Sean smiled at Sally. 'Get on the bike of yours and pedal to the hospital,' he advised, 'because that's where your boyfriend is going to be heading.'

Without pausing to argue, she did as he'd suggested, grabbing her jacket and her helmet and dashing for her mountain bike.

She arrived at the hospital as the helicopter landed, and she sprinted for A and E.

Ben MacAllister, Ellie's husband and one of the A and E consultants, was waiting for the helicopter. 'No guessing why you're here,' he said dryly, holding open the doors so that the crew could wheel the stretcher inside. 'Take him into Resus. And we'll have the boy in that cubicle over there.'

Sally looked at Tom lying on the stretcher with his eyes closed and her heart lurched uncomfortably.

If anything happened to him...

They transferred him across from the stretcher and Sally slid her hand into his. 'Tom?'

His hand felt freezing cold and she warmed it with both of hers, feeling weak-limbed and incredibly shaky.

His eyes opened and he winced slightly. 'What are you doing here? Are you after my body again?'

'I thought I might ravish you while you're under the anaesthetic.' She kept it light. This wasn't the time to have the conversation she wanted to have. 'I didn't have anything else to do. I told Sean I'd keep an eye on you.'

He nodded, a faint smile touching his mouth. 'My leg is killing me.'

'You've cut it.'

'Badly?'

Ben lifted the dressing and examined it. 'Badly enough to give you a scar. Good job you're not a swim-wear model.'

'All I want to know is whether it will ruin my chances of having a decent love life.'

Ben grinned. 'Did you have a decent love life before?' He poked around a bit more and then nodded. 'It's not as bad as I first thought. We can stitch it here. You'll just be a bit sore walking up the aisle with Oliver to-morrow.'

Sally watched as Ben finished his examination, notic-ing how pale Tom looked.

How infinitely precious.

'Were the kids OK in the end?' Tom closed his eyes and his voice sounded weary.

'Thanks to you, I gather.' Ben glanced at the nurse. 'Can I have some more light here, Nicky? It's like work-ing in a cave.'

'Charming.' Nicky, the A and E sister, rolled her eyes

and adjusted the light. 'I happen to prefer romantic lighting myself.'

Ben drew the edges of the laceration together, carefully aligning them to achieve the best result. 'Well, I hate to disappoint you, but I don't fancy Tom.'

Tom smiled, his eyes still closed. 'I'm gutted. Mind you, I'm amazed you can even remember how to talk, married to Ellie. Having just spent a day on the mountain with her, my ears are still ringing. When do you get to practise talking?'

'I practise at work,' Ben said gravely, but his eyes twinkled as he carefully stitched the wound. 'Because obviously at home I can't get a word in edgeways. You're still her hero, by the way.'

'I don't deserve it.'

'Actually, I think you probably do.' Ben's tone was calm. 'Ethan is a wonderful baby and we both know we would have lost him if you hadn't operated so quickly. You didn't hesitate. You got her to Theatre and you got our baby out before the situation had a chance to deteriorate. Other doctors would have hung around and waited.'

Tom still had his eyes closed but Sally thought she saw faint colour touch his hard cheekbones. 'It was the quickest way I knew to stop Ellie talking,' he murmured. 'Anaesthetize her.'

'Well, any time you need your leg sewn up, I'm your man,' Ben said lightly, pushing the stool away and standing up. 'I'm done here. Nicky will dress it more beautifully than I ever could. Take some painkillers, get home to bed and I'll check it at the wedding tomorrow.'

'Can I ride the bike?'

'No.' Ben ripped off his gloves. 'If that's your only option, I'll give you a lift home.'

Tom nodded. 'Thanks. I'd better take you up on that offer.'

Sally felt a flicker of desperation.

There were things she wanted to say to him.

Things she needed to say.

But he was already hobbling after Ben, taking the walking stick that Nicky had jokingly offered him.

Sally followed him to the door, holding it open so that he could pass through, wanting to stop him.

He turned to look at her, his handsome face pale and showing signs of strain. 'Thanks, Sally.' He gave a rueful smile. 'I appreciate the moral support. I'm going to have an early night and see you at the wedding tomorrow.'

She opened her mouth to tell him that she loved him.

To tell him that she wanted to marry him.

But the door had already swung shut behind him.

He was gone.

CHAPTER NINE

'I CAN'T believe I'm standing in this same church, wearing this same suit that doesn't fit properly,' Oliver muttered, sliding a finger round his collar to try and relieve the tension. 'I wanted to get married on the side of a mountain.'

Tom looked at his brother and tried to ignore the throbbing pain in his leg. 'Even you can't expect a woman to exchange vows on the side of a mountain in freezing March.'

'Well, obviously,' Oliver grumbled, 'that's why I agreed to the church. Now I know why Jack was stressed when he got married. Why is she late? Why are brides always late?'

'Calm down.' But Tom's eyes were fixed on the back of the tiny village church as well, although he wasn't interested in the arrival of the bride. Just one of the bridesmaids.

He wanted to see Sally.

Last night, when he'd seen her pale-faced and anxious, waiting for him in the A and E department, he'd been completely swamped by love.

And something far more basic.

He gritted his teeth and shifted uncomfortably. Denying himself was becoming more difficult by the minute, and last night he'd had to get away from her before he gave in to the temptation to take whatever scraps she was offering.

Even an affair had started to look good.

Reminding himself firmly that the sort of affair he wanted lasted for a lifetime, he ran a hand over the back of his neck and looked at his brother. 'Do you want to ask me about my speech?'

Oliver yawned. 'If you're planning to shock the guests, I probably ought to warn you that they already know all my secrets.'

Tom nodded. 'Actually, I wasn't really planning to talk about you at all.'

An idea was beginning to form in his mind.

'I am, after all, only the groom,' Oliver muttered, his tone ironic. Then he caught the look in his brother's eyes and squeezed his shoulder. 'I don't care what you say. We'll all be drunk by then, anyway.'

The organ sounded and Oliver straightened. 'Here we go. And I tell you now, this is positively the last time I'm wearing this suit. When you finally get your act together and marry Sally, you take me as I am.'

Tom glanced over his shoulder, tension rising within him as he saw Helen pause at the top of the aisle.

Behind her was Sally, and Tom caught his breath. She was wearing a slinky green silk dress that hugged her figure and her blonde hair was caught up with delicate flowers.

She looked young and vulnerable and Tom felt his throat close.

How could he ever have let this woman go?

He must have been mad.

Watching them walk down the aisle, his eyes met Sally's and held, refusing to let her look away.

Had Oliver not nudged him sharply he would have totally neglected his duties as best man.

But somehow he managed to get through the ceremony and the photographs, and finally he was in the car with Sally and Bryony on the short journey to the manor house where the reception was being held.

'These shoes are killing me.' Bryony bent down and undid the tiny buckles that fastened the shoes at the ankles. 'How does Helen ever walk in these?'

'I think she's had special training.' Sally laughed, lifting her dress slightly so that she could see her feet. 'I have to confess that I love them, actually.'

Tom swallowed, unable to drag his gaze away from her legs. She was wearing sheer stockings that shimmered temptingly and suddenly he wished that his sister wasn't in the car with them.

'You look beautiful, too, Tom,' Bryony said teasingly. 'Don't you think he looks beautiful, Sal? But you're very quiet, brother, darling. Why are you so quiet?'

Sally looked at him, her green eyes searching. 'Is your leg hurting?'

The concern in her voice filled him with hope. If she was concerned then it must mean that she cared, and if she cared…

'My leg isn't hurting.'

'Perhaps he's nervous about his speech,' Sally said huskily, and suddenly Tom knew exactly what he was going to say in his speech.

And he wasn't nervous at all.

Silence fell over the room as Tom rose to his feet, and the clink of glasses and the laughter gradually faded to nothing.

Watching him from her seat, it occurred to Sally that while Oliver looked jolly uncomfortable in formal dress, Tom looked staggeringly sexy.

But he was a man who would look sexy in nothing.

And she should know.

She looked at his handsome face, listened to the relaxed way that he opened his speech and the way that he had everyone laughing within moments.

Last night she'd wanted so much to tell him that she loved him, but he hadn't given her the chance.

And that was her fault, of course.

She'd rejected him repeatedly. What reason had she ever given him to believe that he could change her mind?

Realizing with a lurch of horror and embarrassment that everyone in the room was suddenly staring at her, she gave a start and glanced towards Tom, wondering what he'd said to make all eyes suddenly settle on hers with speculation.

His blue eyes gleamed with amusement. 'As I was saying,' he continued smoothly, 'one of my duties as best man is to formally thank the bridesmaids and tell them that they look beautiful. So I'll start with my sister. Bryony. You look great. Even if you can't walk in the shoes.'

There was a ripple of laughter around the room and then his gaze focused on Sally.

The silence stretched on and on until gradually the people in the room started to look at each other with puzzled expressions, wondering what was happening.

When he finally spoke, his voice was for everyone but his eyes were only for her.

'And now I want to tell you something about Sally, apart from the fact that she looks great in her dress. Most of you probably know that I ended my relationship with Sally seven years ago.' His voice was slightly hoarse and he cleared his throat, totally indifferent to the sudden rapt attention of everyone in the room. 'What you probably don't know is that I've regretted it every day since.

I thought she was too young to settle down. I was wrong. I thought that she needed space. I was wrong. I thought that I knew better than she did what she needed, and I was wrong about that, too.'

There was total silence in the room and Sally felt a few eyes turn in her direction but her own gaze was still locked on Tom's.

An odd smile played around his firm mouth. 'I was wrong about a lot of things. But most of all I was wrong about how much she meant to me. By the time I discovered that she meant everything, it was too late because I'd already damaged our relationship. Perhaps beyond repair.' He took a deep breath and finally dragged his gaze away from Sally and looked at his audience. 'You're probably asking yourselves why I'm admitting this in public. I'm going to tell you why. This is a small community and every time Sally and I look at each other someone decides that we should be back together. So I'm doing this in public, once and for all, so that everyone can know what the score is.'

Sally's heart was thumping so hard that she thought she might pass out.

His blue eyes were warm on hers. 'Sally—it's traditional for the best man to give the bridesmaid a gift. Will you come here, please?'

Her legs shaking, she somehow got to her feet and managed to walk the few paces towards him.

He held out a tiny box.

'This is my gift to you, Sally.' He spoke clearly, so that everyone in the room could hear what he was saying. 'I love you. I will always love you and while there is still breath in my body I will always be here for you. I want you to marry me. And I'm asking you in public whether our relationship is beyond repair. Last time I made the decision for both of us and I was wrong. Now I'm asking you to make the decision for yourself. Will you marry me?'

Her hands were shaking so much that she couldn't open the box. He took it gently from her and flipped open the lid with a finger.

A gorgeous emerald, the exact colour of her dress, gleamed in a diamond setting and she gasped.

'Oh, Tom!'

He stepped closer still, lowered his voice, and this time his words were only for her. 'I love you, angel, with all my heart. Marry me and I'll spend the rest of my life proving that you can trust me.'

He lifted the ring out of its box and there was an agonized silence while everyone looked at Sally expectantly.

The hush in the room was almost deafening.

'I love you, too.' Her voice was little more than a whisper but he caught the words and a satisfied smile spread across his handsome face.

'In that case, Sally soon-to-be-Hunter, you'd better wear that ring.'

As soon as they saw him sliding the ring onto her finger, there were loud cheers and catcalls and shrieks of, 'You may kiss the bridesmaid.'

Tom did as he was ordered and Sally melted against him, feeling his mouth on hers.

Then she remembered where she was and pulled away, glancing around self-consciously.

'This is Oliver and Helen's wedding.'

Helen was by her side, clutching her arm in delight and excitement. 'Oh, don't apologize! That was the nicest wedding speech I've ever heard,' she said dreamily, mopping the tears from her eyes, 'and absolutely no one has fallen asleep.'

'It suited me, too,' Oliver muttered, reaching for his champagne. 'Better than all those dull stories about my drunken student days.'

Tom smiled and led Sally away from the table and out of the room, leaving the others to their champagne and gossip.

'Where are we going?'

'Somewhere where we can talk in peace without an audience. I don't mind proposing in public but I draw the line at having observers for the next bit.'

He pulled her into a small library where a log fire burned and closed the door, turning the key in the lock.

'There are still things that haven't been said. Let's start with why you waited up half the night at the rescue centre and then cycled to the hospital.'

She couldn't stop looking at the ring that glittered on her finger. She twisted it, staring down at her finger in awe.

A feeling of perfect happiness spread through her and she lifted her eyes to his, unable to resist teasing him just a little. 'I waited at the rescue centre because I wanted to keep Sean company.'

His blue eyes gleamed. 'That's what I thought. And you cycled to the hospital because you thought Ben wouldn't be able to stitch me up without your help.'

She fiddled with the ring again. 'Sounds about right. And I also thought that, given you were injured, I might be able to have my evil way with your body.'

He laughed. 'So now the truth is out. Even though I was injured, all you could think about was seducing me.'

'I'm afraid so.'

'You had designs on my body.'

'I've had designs on your body since I found out what a boy's body is for,' she murmured softly, her smile all woman as she finally looked at him. 'Is it my fault if you're a bit slow?'

His eyes narrowed. 'Last night in the hospital…'

'I wanted to tell you that I loved you.' Her voice was soft. 'But we were surrounded by people and then you seemed so desperate to get away from me.'

He gave a wry smile. 'I'd reached the point where I could no longer be in the same room as you and not commit an indecent act.'

She gave a chuckle. 'In that case, I'm glad you just locked that door.'

He slid his hands round her face. 'I love you, Sally Jenner.' His voice rang with sincerity. 'Do you believe me?'

'Yes.' She nodded. 'And I love you, too.'

He closed his eyes and breathed out heavily. 'I never thought I'd get you to admit that again. You used to say it to me all the time, and you have no idea how much I missed hearing those words from you.'

'And I missed saying them.'

His mouth came down on hers and he kissed her gently. 'Am I allowed to know what changed your mind, or was it just an intolerable increase in your levels of sexual frustration?'

She smiled, stroking a finger over his rough jaw. 'I suppose you should thank Sean.'

He frowned. 'Sean?'

'I never doubted that I loved you, Tom,' she said softly, 'I just doubted that I could give all of myself to you again. I was afraid to risk rejection for a second time.'

'And what did Sean have to do with that?'

'He pointed out that risk plays a part in so much of life, especially the parts that we especially value.' She slipped her fingers inside the buttons of his shirt and heard his sharp intake of breath. 'And right now we're standing in a library with one hundred and fifty guests less than a shout away. Just how much of a risk taker are you, Tom Hunter?'

He gave a slow smile and brought his mouth down on hers, unzipping her dress with a skill that would have earned admiration from James Bond.

'I've always been a risk taker, as you know.' His voice was husky as he backed her towards the sofa. 'And I don't intend to stop now.'

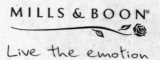

MILLS & BOON®

Live the emotion

His Boardroom Mistress

In February 2005 By Request brings
back three favourite novels by our
bestselling Mills & Boon authors:

The Husband Assignment
by Helen Bianchin
The Baby Verdict *by Cathy Williams*
The Bedroom Business *by Sandra Marton*

Seduction from 9-5...
and after hours!

On sale 4th February 2005

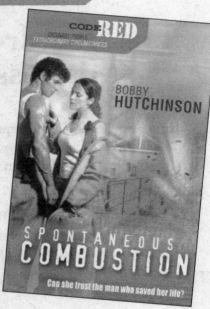

4 FREE

BOOKS AND A SURPRISE GIFT!

We would like to take this opportunity to thank you for reading this Mills & Boon® book by offering you the chance to take FOUR more specially selected titles from the Medical Romance™ series absolutely FREE! We're also making this offer to introduce you to the benefits of the Reader Service™—

- ★ **FREE home delivery**
- ★ **FREE gifts and competitions**
- ★ **FREE monthly Newsletter**
- ★ **Exclusive Reader Service offers**
- ★ **Books available before they're in the shops**

Accepting these FREE books and gift places you under no obligation to buy, you may cancel at any time, even after receiving your free shipment. Simply complete your details below and return the entire page to the address below. You don't even need a stamp!

YES! Please send me 4 free Medical Romance books and a surprise gift. I understand that unless you hear from me, I will receive 6 superb new titles every month for just £2.69 each, postage and packing free. I am under no obligation to purchase any books and may cancel my subscription at any time. The free books and gift will be mine to keep in any case.

M5ZED

Ms/Mrs/Miss/Mr ....Initials ....
BLOCK CAPITALS PLEASE

Surname ....

Address ....

....

....Postcode........................

Send this whole page to:
UK: FREEPOST CN81, Croydon, CR9 3WZ.